JOURNEY INTO WAR

Margaret Donaldson

Illustrated by Joanna Stubbs

Hippo Books
Scholastic Publications Ltd
London

Scholastic Publications Ltd,
161 Fulham Road, London SW3 6SW England

Scholastic Book Services,
50 West 44th Street, New York 10036 NY USA

Scholastic Tab Publications Ltd,
123 Newkirk Road, Richmond Hill, Ontario L4C 3G5
Canada

H J Ashton Co Pty Ltd, Box 579,
Gosford, New South Wales, Australia

H J Ashton Co Pty Ltd,
9–11 Fairfax Avenue, Penrose, Auckland, New Zealand

First published by André Deutsch Ltd 1979
Published by Scholastic Publications Ltd 1980
Copyright © 1979 by Margaret Donaldson
All rights reserved

Typeset by Computacomp (UK) Ltd, Fort William,
Scotland
Made and printed in the U.S.A.
Set in Baskerville

Journey Into War

It is May, 1940, and France is about to fall
to the German Army. Ten-year-old Janey
has been in France for two years, but now
her father insists that she should go back
to England. In the care of Martin, the
gardener, she is on her way to Dieppe
when they get separated and Janey is
stranded, alone. There is only one thing
she can do. She must try and get to St
Quentin and find her father.

So, with a horse to ride, and a dog for
company, she sets off only to find her
father has left and the town is in the hands
of the Germans.

Janey doesn't know where to turn or
what to do, until she meets up with two
Polish boys, also stranded. Together they
decide to wage their own war against the
Germans, but it is a war they cannot win.
When they try to put the German trucks
out of action Janey is captured by the
Gestapo, and it is only with the help of a
sympathetic German officer that the twins
have a chance of rescuing her. But can
Lieutenant Werner be genuine? Can the
boys trust him ...?

An exciting wartime adventure story for
readers of 9 and over.

Chapter 1

Janey heard the roar of the aeroplane engines and turned to look over her shoulder. Martin took his eyes off the crowded road just long enough to do the same. They saw the machine heading straight towards them from the north-east, flying low over the fields.

Martin pulled the car sharply on to the grass by the roadside and stopped it so suddenly that Janey's neck was jerked painfully and her head hit the windscreen.

'Oh!' she cried. 'What ...'

But Martin had no time to listen.

'Out!' he yelled. 'Into the ditch! Quick!'

All along the road other people were running for shelter too. Janey scrambled out, leaving the door wide open. She reached the ditch with Martin close behind her, just as the plane crossed a clump of trees about a hundred yards away. The sun gleamed on its wings, but you could not see the markings.

Apart from these trees, the flat French countryside was bare and open. The ditch was the only possible hiding place.

'Right down!' said Martin. 'Keep your head right down! Lie still!'

Janey slid down through the grass and lay at the bottom. She got a mouthful of dry dust and she twisted her head, trying to spit it out. Pain shot up from her shoulder like fire. She had forgotten about her neck. She groaned and rubbed it.

Martin was in the ditch too now, doing his best to shield her with his broad shoulders. The noise grew louder, deafening. Janey covered her ears with her hands, but nothing could keep it out. The plane roared directly above them and seemed to stay still there for a second, filling the sky. Then the throb of its engines began to fade away to the south-west.

Martin got up and brushed the dust off his clothes. He pushed his thin hair out of his eyes.

'All right now,' he said. 'It's gone.'

They walked back slowly to the car.

'Was it a German plane?' asked Janey.

'I don't know,' said Martin. 'I didn't see the markings on the wings. I don't know much about aeroplanes. I am too old to want to learn such things.'

He helped Janey to climb back into the car and he shut the door for her.

'I expect it was a French plane or a British one,' he said as he climbed in himself and started the engine.

'Yes,' said Janey. 'It would have shot at us if it had been German, wouldn't it?'

Martin glanced sideways at her but he did not answer.

All along the road other people were

8

coming out of the ditch and starting their engines or whipping up their horses. Many of them were driving farm wagons or old carts instead of cars. The wagons were loaded like removal vans. Janey had never seen such a strange sight.

Just in front of them a woman was lifting two young children up into a cart which was piled high with furniture and blankets, so that the children had to perch on top of the pile. Janey could hear the woman speaking to the older child in a voice that was sharp with fear. 'Hold on to your little brother! Hold on to him tightly now, so that he doesn't fall!' The younger child was sucking his thumb and crying. The woman rubbed her hand across her tired face, leaving a dirty mark on her brow.

Martin pulled the car out on to the road and they began to drive westwards again. Janey looked at her watch. It was half past five. The sun was dropping lower in the sky now and it was shining in Martin's eyes. He put on his dark glasses. Janey noticed that his hand was shaking.

They reached the town of Clermont about thirty minutes later, but took a long time to get through it for the traffic was worse than ever. There were more farm carts now and every one of them was loaded with furniture and luggage. In some of the carts whole families were sitting on top of the luggage in the shade of large umbrellas. There were hens in crates and cows tied to the wagons by ropes and following behind.

Martin spoke to a policeman while they were stuck in the traffic. He asked for news. The policeman frowned.

'Bad,' he said. 'These people who are crowding the road from Amiens say that the Germans have reached St Quentin.'

Martin shook his head.

'We left St Quentin less than three hours ago,' he said. 'The Germans are not there yet.'

The policeman shrugged his shoulders.

'You don't know what to believe,' he said. He looked at Janey. 'Where are you taking this child?' he asked.

'To Dieppe,' answered Martin. 'She's English. She has been living with her father in France for two years since her mother died. Today he decided she must go home.'

'Not a day too soon,' said the policeman. 'The Germans don't love the English, that's sure.' He waved them on, as the cart in front lurched forward. They took the road to Beauvais.

For a while Janey sat quite still. Martin did not speak either.

'Do you hate the Germans?' Janey asked him at last.

'Yes, I hate them.'

'Why do you hate them?'

'Because they are attacking France and killing us,' said Martin. 'Is that not a good reason?'

Janey thought this over for a bit. Then: 'Do you hate the English?' she asked.

Martin raised his eyebrows.

'No!' he said. 'Why should I do that?'

'Once they attacked the French and killed them too,' she said. 'Don't you know about Joan of Arc?'

Martin laughed.

'But that's all over now,' he said. 'That was long ago.'

'I'm glad you don't hate us now, Martin,' said Janey. 'Will you not hate the Germans either when the war is over?'

Martin stopped smiling.

'I suppose we may forgive them some day,' he said, 'but that will take a little while.'

The road seemed to grow busier all the time. There were many army trucks now, loaded with soldiers, but most of them were British. Janey could tell by the uniforms. She thought how strange it would be to be back in England, going to an English school, not speaking French any more.

It was growing late and still they had not reached Beauvais. They were moving slowly behind an old rusty van, with three huge fat mattresses strapped across its roof. The ropes were not tight enough and the mattresses were slowly sliding down the left side. Martin could not see anything in front because of the mattresses and so he could not get past this van. He was beginning to look worried. He glanced at his watch.

'Are we going to miss the boat?' asked Janey.

'I hope not!' said Martin. He blew his horn very loudly and for a long time.

When he stopped, Janey heard another

noise. It was a kind of spluttering sound and it came from the engine.

Martin said some very rude words in French. Janey knew they were rude although she was not quite sure what they meant.

The engine spluttered worse than ever and the car moved very slowly. Now other drivers behind them were beginning to blow *their* horns.

Martin turned into a lane that led to the yard of a small farmhouse. He stopped the engine and then got out and peered at it. Janey got out and peered at it too. It looked quite ordinary to both of them, so Martin tried to start it again. Nothing happened.

'I'm a gardener,' he said, 'not a mechanic. I can't fix this thing. I'll have to go and look for someone who knows about cars. And you'll have to stay here till I get back.'

'I'd rather come too,' said Janey.

'You can't walk fast enough,' Martin told her. 'And you'd get tired too quickly. Come on! Let's see who lives in this house.'

They crossed the yard and knocked on the door. No one came. Martin knocked again. Then Janey saw an old woman's face peering at them through a dirty window.

'Look, Martin!' she said, but the face vanished before he could turn. 'I saw a woman,' she told him.

'If she won't let you in, I suppose you will have to come with me,' he said. But just at that moment the door opened slowly and the woman asked: 'What do you want?' in a voice that sounded frightened and tired.

Martin explained about the car.

'The little girl is English but she speaks good French,' he said. 'And I will pay you good French money to look after her till I get back.'

The woman's eyes flitted across to the car. 'When will you be back?' she asked.

'Tonight, with luck,' said Martin. 'To-morrow morning at the latest. I'll go to the nearest garage and fetch a mechanic.'

The old woman started to cough very badly but she managed to ask: 'How much money?'

'Fifteen francs if I come back tonight. Thirty if you keep her till tomorrow.'

'Not enough,' said the old woman, still struggling with her cough. 'Forty if it's tonight and sixty if it's tomorrow.'

'All right,' Martin agreed with a sigh, 'though you know very well it's robbery. Forty or sixty! See that you feed her well!'

He fetched Janey's suitcase and her canvas bag from the car and carried them into the house.

'I'll be back as soon as I can, Janey,' he told her. Then he turned to the old woman. 'Thirty francs for you now,' he said. 'The rest when I get back if you've looked after the child well.' And he gave her the money and went away. Janey stood by the window watching him. He walked with long strides, for he was a big man and he was hurrying. His shoulders were hunched, his head was thrust forward. He looked like some great bird, anxious for the safety of its babies.

A small vegetable patch and an apple tree lay between the yard and the road. Janey's eyes followed Martin as he went down the lane and turned right. She went on watching him as he passed behind the apple tree and over a bridge that crossed a little stream. Then, as his figure grew smaller and was lost among the other shapes still fleeing along that shadowy road, Janey was hit by a new wave of fear. This fear was a cold, shaky feeling that she had not known before—not even in the ditch with the aeroplane overhead. She leaned her brow against the window pane and closed her eyes.

The old woman sat down in a rocking chair and looked at Janey's back.

'What's your name, child?' she said. 'How old are you?'

Janey said that she was called Jeanne, for that was the nearest you could get to her name in French. She added that she was ten years old. The old woman began to talk, but she was really talking to herself, not to Janey.

'What a world!' she said. 'What a world! The dirty Germans coming again! Can't an old woman live in peace? Where's that son of mine? He promised to come and take me away to Brittany, but there's no sign of him. What will happen to me if I'm still sitting here all alone when the German tanks come down that road, eh? What will happen to me? Eh? Where's that son of mine?'

In between words she coughed and spluttered. The rocking chair creaked as she swung it to and fro. A cat with yellowish fur jumped up on to her lap. It looked old and tired like the woman.

A big convoy of army trucks was moving along the road, going eastwards. Janey, too, began to wonder what would happen if the British and the French soldiers weren't there and the German ones came instead. She watched the road and held her breath.

Chapter 2

It got quite dark. The old woman lit two
candles. Then she put a big fat loaf of bread
on the table and served some thick soup.
After that they each had a slice of ham. The
old woman drank red wine and gave Janey a
little, mixed with a lot of water.

By the end of the meal Martin had not
returned.

'You'll be here all night, child,' said the
old woman. 'He'll not find a mechanic
before the morning. Come with me.'

She picked up a candle and began to walk
to the kitchen door. Then she stopped
suddenly, as if she had only just thought of
something.

'What if he never comes back?' she said,
thrusting the candle towards Janey's face and
peering at her. 'That would be a fine trick to
play on an old woman! Dumping a child on
me! That's one way to get rid of a problem.
But I won't keep you—don't you think I
will!'

Janey was suddenly hot with anger. 'He
will come back,' she said. 'And I wouldn't
stay with you anyway.'

The old woman began to cough again,

worse than ever, as she led Janey to a very small room at the back of the house. The room was almost completely filled by an enormous bed with a big bulging mattress like the ones on the back of the van they had been following. There were no pillows but there was a fat round bolster without a cover.

Janey climbed into bed and sank deep into the mattress. There was only one blanket but she hardly needed even that, for the night was warm. Her body was aching with tiredness now, but she could not sleep. She twisted and wriggled restlessly, as her mind went back over that strange day.

She remembered the morning. It had been an ordinary morning at first, just like all the others, with the sun shining calmly through the bedroom window when Marianne came to waken her. But Marianne seemed to be in a funny mood at breakfast-time and at school you could tell that something was wrong. The teacher's face was pale and she kept looking out of the window. Her hand shook when she tried to write on the blackboard—just the way Martin's had done, thought Janey, remembering. After an hour or so in school, a boy from another class came in with a note. The teacher read it and sent the children home without telling them why. But she said several times: 'You must go straight home to your parents. You must not go and play.' This was all very puzzling. But Marianne also refused to explain.

The next strange thing was that Janey's father came home at lunch time. Usually he was not back until late at night. For just a moment, as she heard the car coming up the drive, Janey hoped that he had a holiday too and that they could go fishing together. But as soon as she looked at his face she knew that he had come home for a different reason.

At least he was willing to tell her what was happening. 'Janey,' he said, 'I have to send you back to England. The Germans are too near. It's not safe for you to stay.'

Janey knew there was a war. She had often seen soldiers and tanks and guns moving up and down the roads, but they were always friendly soldiers who waved and smiled. The fighting seemed to be far away. No one was worried about it. Now suddenly everyone was worried. Something had changed.

'Are the Germans winning?' she asked her father quite calmly.

He nodded. 'It looks like it just now,' he answered. 'But don't worry, Janey. We'll beat them in the end.'

Suddenly she thought of leaving him and she couldn't keep calm any longer. 'I won't go without you,' she cried. 'I won't! Please come too!' But he told her firmly that he would have to stay longer in St Quentin, for he still had work to finish. 'I'll be with you again soon,' he promised. So Martin came with another car and took her away. He had been planning to put her on a boat at Dieppe. Her Aunt Sarah was going to meet her at Newhaven in the morning.

Now she was all alone in a dark French cottage with a funny cross old woman. And the Germans might come along the road. They might even come before the morning and break the door down. Janey did not know what would happen after that. Would they take her away to a prison? Or would they shoot her? She shivered and listened for the rumbling of their engines and the thump of their heavy feet. But there was no sound at all in the darkness. In the end she fell asleep.

Janey woke with a jump next morning, wondering where she was. As soon as she remembered, she scrambled out of the big bed and ran to look for Martin, feeling sure he would be back. But the old woman was alone in the kitchen, lighting the fire. Martin had not come.

The old woman gave her some bread and a bowl of coffee to drink. But she muttered crossly all the time, saying that thirty francs wouldn't last long with the price of things these days, and food scarce and sure to get scarcer—and what was to happen with the dirty Germans coming again?

As soon as she could get out of the house, Janey went to the end of the lane and sat on the fence, watching the road. It was just the same as yesterday. There was an endless stream of traffic moving westwards, with hardly anyone going the other way. She told herself that this was good, for when Martin came back from Beauvais with the mechanic he would be able to travel easily and quickly.

Janey searched for Martin through every gap between the cars and the trucks and the wagons. She searched till her eyes ached. She told herself that by the time she had counted twenty he would be there. But she counted to twenty hundreds of times and still his tall figure did not appear.

Half-way through the morning she heard the old woman shouting and she ran back to the house. 'At least you can help a bit,' the old woman said, and she gave Janey a hatchet and told her to chop up some firewood. Janey did this till her arms hurt, but she did not mind. She was glad to have something to do.

By lunch time, Martin had still not come. 'I told you so,' said the old woman in a nasty sort of way. She did not give Janey very much to eat. But it did not matter. Janey was hardly able to eat what she got.

In the early afternoon she went out to the road again and tried to think what to do. Everything would be all right, of course, if only her father knew what had happened, for he would come at once to fetch her. So she should phone him! She raced back at once to the farmhouse. But there was no telephone there, which was not at all surprising. She would just have to set out and find one.

'How far is it to Beauvais?' she asked, for there was sure to be a telephone at the post office there. The old woman's face grew brighter when she heard the question. She answered: 'About two kilometres.'

'I'm going to telephone my father,' said Janey. 'Perhaps I'll meet Martin on the way.'

The old woman nodded and managed to look almost pleased. The yellowish cat rubbed itself against Janey's legs and she stroked it, although she did not like it much. Then she set off westwards along the road to Beauvais.

She kept to the left-hand side so that she would be sure to see Martin—or rather so that he would be sure to see her. This meant that she was in the full heat of the sun all the time, missing the chance to rest for a moment or two in the shade of one of the tall poplar trees that lined the right-hand verge. It couldn't be helped.

After about half an hour she came to a signpost which said: Beauvais, 5 kilometres. She sighed. It was clear that the old woman had told her a lie so as to encourage her to go. But there was no question of turning back.

No one asked her if she would like to ride on a cart for a while. All the cars and trucks were packed full of people and their belongings, and all the people were in a hurry. Their faces looked hard and tight. They took no notice of her at all.

However, she was not the only one who was walking. Some of the people had prams and children with them, or carts that they were pushing. Janey helped one woman with three little children to push her cart along the last half-mile of the hot dusty road into Beauvais. The woman had come a long way from a place far in the north (afterwards Janey could never remember its name) and she was trying to get to her father's house in Normandy. She was very tired.

Soon after Janey had left the farmhouse, a man rode into the yard on a bicycle. But it was not Martin, it was the old woman's son. He had come to keep his promise and take her away. He was planning to load her cart with as many things as possible, harness the horse and drive to Brittany. 'But the poor beast will probably drop dead before we get there,' he said. Then he saw the big grey car and his eyes gleamed.

'Where did that come from?' he asked.

His mother told him. The man went over and looked at the engine. After a minute he rolled up his sleeves and began fiddling with

it. After about ten minutes it started with a roar.

'Right!' he said. 'We're taking this. Hurry up now. What's to go?'

The old woman looked uneasy. Then she said: 'Oh, well, why not? That man will never come back, anyway.' And she began to help her son to pile things into the car and tie things on to the roof. By the time Janey had reached the post office in Beauvais they were ready to drive away.

'Don't go through Beauvais,' said the old woman. They turned south and headed for Pontoise.

The man at the post office shook his head. 'We can't reach St Quentin,' he said. 'The lines seem to be cut. There's no way.'

'Please,' said Janey. 'Please can't you ...'

'Listen, child,' said the man. 'If the lines are down I can't get a call through. Don't you understand?'

'I'll have to go there, then,' said Janey. 'Please, where is the railway station?'

'There'll be no more trains going to the north now,' he told her. 'Don't you understand? The Germans are up there.' Then he pushed his spectacles up on to his forehead and looked at Janey's face. 'Are you all alone, child?' he asked.

'No, no,' Janey answered quickly. 'Martin will be back. Thank you.'

She went outside again and stood at the top of the steps, leaning against the wall. She felt tears coming into her eyes and she found that she was sobbing.

The post office stood on the corner of a wide street that ran through the town from north to south and led in the direction of the main road to Paris. So of course the street was crowded. Janey could not bear the sight of these hurrying people any longer. She turned into a quieter side street, brushed her tears away and found a little café that was still open. There seemed to be no other customers.

She ordered a chocolate icecream and sat at a table outside the café while she ate it. The man who served her wiped the table top and said: 'You should go home at once. It is not a time for children to be out alone. Who knows what will happen?' She nodded but she did not reply.

When she had finished the icecream she

paid the man with a five-franc piece and he went inside to bring her change. Then, as she sat there waiting for him, feeling helpless and close to despair, she happened to glance sideways and her heart gave a sudden leap that made her catch her breath. For a man had just come out of a doorway farther along the street—a tall man with familiar-looking hunched shoulders—Martin!

She did not see the man's face for he was moving in the other direction, away from her. 'Martin!' she shouted, and ran after him. But he was already turning the corner.

'Hey!' shouted the waiter behind her. 'Your change, miss!' Janey scarcely heard him. She was running at top speed, with her heart pounding against her ribs, full of fear that Martin would vanish again. But in the next street there he was, only a few yards away, standing still, bending his head to light a cigarette. 'Martin!' she cried joyfully.

The man turned to look at her with the cigarette between his lips, the lighted match still in his hand, surprise in his eyes. It was a face that Janey had never seen in her life before.

She managed to stop before she had quite bumped into him. For a moment she stood there gaping at him. His face looked ugly to her, and terrifying. He had a big red nose and pale blue eyes that bulged at her behind thick spectacles. She gave one little gasping cry before she turned and ran away from him.

The man stared after her. His eyes were

kind really, if you took the time to look at them and if you did not expect him to be Martin. The match began to burn his fingers. He dropped it quickly, struck another one and got the cigarette lit at last. Then he shrugged his shoulders, hunched them up again and walked away.

Afterwards, Janey did not remember very clearly how she found her way to the road that led back to the old woman's cottage. But she did come to it in the end, and there seemed to be nothing else that she could do except walk back along it.

Now she was very tired and her feet hurt. She moved slowly and rested sometimes. It would have been good to go to sleep by the roadside, but always she made herself get up and forced herself to struggle on. For after all there was still the faint hope that Martin would be there when she got back, waiting for her.

When she reached the little bridge at last and could see into the yard of the farmhouse, the first thing she looked for was the car. It was gone! The space where it had stood at the end of the lane was empty except for an old wooden box and a cigarette packet that had been tossed carelessly away.

Chapter 3

After the first moment of shock, Janey decided it was good that the car was not there. 'That means Martin came back with a mechanic,' she thought. 'He must have got the car started and then gone to look for me and missed me. He'll be here again soon.'

But there was something odd. All the shutters on the windows were closed, though it was only half-past eight. She listened to her watch to make sure it had not stopped, but in any case the sky was still light. She limped up the lane and knocked on the front door.

There was no answer. After a while she went to the back of the house and knocked again. Still there was no answer, and all the shutters were closed there too.

Janey stepped back one or two paces and looked at the house in despair. Then she jumped forward again and banged on the door with both fists, yelling, 'Let me in!' For she thought at first that the old woman was still inside and had decided to lock her out so as to get rid of her. But when she was quite exhausted by banging on the door she suddenly remembered about the old woman's son.

'So that's it!' Janey thought. 'He came—and they've gone!' But she still did not begin to suspect that they had taken the car, and she told herself that Martin was sure to be back with it before long. So the only thing to do was to wait for him.

There was a water tap on the wall at the back of the house. She drank from it and splashed the water over her feet. That felt very good. Then she went to the front again and sat down with her back against the apple tree. In ten minutes she was curled up on the ground, fast asleep.

When she opened her eyes the stars were shining brightly in the sky. She shivered and yawned and raised herself on one elbow. A car came round the corner with its headlights on. As Janey turned away from the glare of it, her eyes met two bright green gleaming things, not much more than a yard away. She did not know what they were at first, but she felt her hair rising on her scalp in fear. Then the bright things vanished and, where they had been, she saw the dark shape of a huge dog. It seemed to be crouching, ready to spring.

Janey opened her mouth and screamed. The dog disappeared behind a tree.

Janey's whole body was shaking now. She could not get the trembling to stop. She peered around her into the darkness.

There was no light or movement from the house and there was still no car in the lane. Janey looked up at the closed shutters and decided that she must break in. She was not sure if she had seen a real dog or the ghost of a dog, but she knew that she could not stay out in the dark night beside it, whatever it was.

She remembered the hatchet which she had used to chop the firewood that morning. It was just possible that the old woman had left it lying outside when she went away.

Janey picked herself up from the ground and crept over towards the pile of logs, looking around her all the time in case the monstrous figure of the dog should appear again. Then she groped for the hatchet in the darkness. Her imagination had been so stirred by the sight of the dog that she was full of fear in case her hands might touch something horrible—something slimy or something that would bite. So, even when her fingers found something firm and cold and hard, she gave another little gasp of alarm before she made certain that it was the hatchet blade.

Once she was sure of this, she drew a deep breath and began to feel better. She reached for the handle, picked it up and went to the back of the house, gripping it tightly in both hands. It was easy to find the little room where she had slept the night before.

She swung the hatchet and began to smash the shutter.

Although she was small and thin, her fear made her strong. Also the wood had not been painted for a long time and parts of it were quite rotten. It snapped and splintered with a satisfying noise. She bit her lip and

smashed it harder than ever until fragments
fell away and the broken shutter swung loose
on one hinge.

Janey stepped back, took a deep breath
and looked at it with pride. Then she
climbed on to the sill and tried to open the
window. But she could not get it to move. So
she held the hatchet firmly again and
smashed one pane. She knocked the glass out
carefully where it was all jagged near the
edge of the wood, and she brushed the pieces
off the window sill. While she worked, she
looked over her shoulder every few seconds
in case the dog might come, but there was
no sign of him.

When the glass was cleared away, she
climbed through the window. She got one
small cut on her left hand. She sucked it.

The house was very dark. She left the bedroom, shutting the door carefully behind her because of the dog. 'If he's a real dog,' she thought, 'he won't get through there. And if he's a ghost ...' She shrugged her shoulders. 'Well, if he's a ghost there's no way to keep him out and I don't suppose ghost dogs can bite you anyway.' It was amazing how much braver she felt now. Everything seemed better since she had taken the hatchet and smashed that shutter.

She went into the kitchen and groped for candles in the darkness but could not find any. So she decided to sit in the rocking chair until the morning and make plans. She tucked her legs up under her and sucked her finger where it had been cut and swung herself to and fro and tried to think what to do.

She could not wait for Martin any longer. She knew he had meant to come back for her, but it was clear now that something had gone wrong. If she just waited here, then the German soldiers might come down the road instead of him.

It seemed to Janey that she had to try to get home to her father. The man in the post office had said there would be no more trains. Well, then, she supposed she could walk, though she knew it would take many days. She decided that she would keep off the road, which she hated now, and go across the fields instead. Then she would be less likely to meet the Germans on the way. She would take the hatchet with her, and some food and some water. If she found other houses that were empty she would break into them and sleep there. Janey knew she would never have dreamed of doing such a thing in peacetime, but now it was war and it seemed to her that everything had changed.

By the time she had made up her mind, light was beginning to shine faintly through the chinks in the shutters. She went over to the window, opened it, thrust the shutters back and let the day pour freely into the room.

The first thing was to look for food, but it was no surprise to find that the larder had been cleared out. The only things left were a big bone with some meat still on it and a few scraps of cheese. The old woman had not bothered to take these with her and she had been hurrying so much that she had forgotten to throw them away. The fat brown milk jug was empty.

Janey turned next to her canvas bag, and that was better. Marianne had put chocolate and apples in it. There were also four boiled eggs, and there was a bit of bread, though it was hard now and stale. Janey ate two of the eggs and some of the bread and wished she had a glass of milk to drink. Just at that moment she heard a cow lowing in the field outside.

Janey had helped to milk a cow twice before in her life, when Marianne had taken her to the little farm near St Quentin where her mother lived. She decided now to try it on her own.

The back door was locked and the key was not there, so she climbed out again through the broken window.

It was a still, clear morning. The early sunlight came slanting across the farmyard, gleaming on the tiny drops of dew that were strung along the wires of the fence. It was good to come out from the dark stuffy house. She took a deep breath of the cool air.

Then she saw the dog. He rose slowly from the place where he was lying, over beside the cowshed. He was very big and brown and shaggy-looking. He put his head down and eyed her. Janey backed against the wall.

The next instant the dog barked and raced across the yard. She just had time to clamber on to the windowsill before he reached her.

She had one leg inside the window when she looked back and saw his wagging tail.

Janey laughed then, but she was still nervous when he tried to jump up. It took some time for her to find the courage to climb out again and go to fetch the cow. The dog trotted beside her, all quiet now, while she brought the cow into the shed, found a pail and started to do the milking. Her fingers were clumsy and the milk did not flow easily, but she got more than she could drink. She poured the rest into a dish for the dog and she brought the bone from the larder for him. While he gnawed it eagerly, Janey watched him and wondered where he came from. And she wondered who would milk the cow when she had gone away.

The next thing was to pack the canvas bag. Janey put in a sharp knife as well as the hatchet, but it was the hatchet that seemed specially important to her. She also packed matches and some candles and a bottle of water. Then she added a saucepan. It was the smallest she could find, but it was made of iron and it was very heavy.

She was wearing a light pair of sandals. She took them off and put on the strongest pair of shoes she could find in the suitcase which Martin had carried into the house for her. She also took a warm sweater and stuffed it into the top of the bag.

The last things that she packed were her British passport and the money her father had given her.

She had a diary with a little pencil in a

leather holder. She tore out a page and left a message for Martin on the kitchen table.

Dear Martin,
    I waited for you but you did not come. I know you couldn't help it. I am going back home. I am going to walk across the fields. I don't want to meet the Germans on the road.

                           Love,
                          Janey

Inside the back cover of the diary there was a map of France folded up small. Janey opened it and looked at it carefully. It did not give much detail, but she could see Beauvais marked, and Clermont and Compiègne and St Quentin. They lay like this:

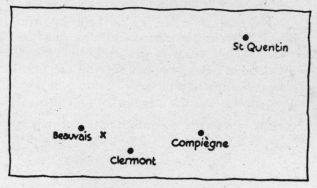

Janey was at the place marked X. She had to travel northeast to get home. She had no compass but she knew how to find where the south was. She knew that she must point the hour hand of her watch towards the sun and then go on halfway round between there and one o'clock on the watch dial.* That would be south. Then north would be directly opposite, east would be on her right hand if she faced the north—and of course north-east would be halfway between.

She picked up the bag and climbed through the window. 'That's the last time I'll be in there,' she thought with pleasure. Then she stood in the yard working out which way to go. It turned out that if she went north-east she would have to go through a village which straggled up from the road not far away. She wanted to avoid all villages as far as she could, so she decided to go north first and then turn eastwards later. But she stood for a moment looking to the north-east past the trees and the red rooftops and thinking that far away over there, beyond the horizon, was home.

It was now nine o'clock on Saturday, the 18th of May. If her eyes could have reached as far as the gateway of her home, Janey would have seen the first of the German tanks passing it at that very moment as they rolled along into the town of St Quentin.

* In May 1940 there was one hour of summertime in France. So the sun would be due south at one o'clock.

Chapter 4

Janey climbed the fence. She was beginning to admit to herself already that the bag would be heavy for her to carry. The grey horse was in the field grazing. Janey thought that horses were lucky, for even in a war there was grass to eat and they didn't have to go hungry or carry their food and things in heavy bags. Of course a bag wouldn't seem heavy to them anyway!

Janey stopped walking suddenly, for she had had an idea. Why not ride home?

She hung her bag on a fence post and ran to search for reins and a saddle in the outhouses of the farm. She found the reins easily but there was no saddle anywhere that she could see. A blanket would have to do instead. She climbed back through the window once again, and fetched two blankets instead of one, for she thought they would keep her warm if the weather grew colder. Then she fixed the reins to the horse's halter, threw the blankets over his back and led him to the fence, where she mounted him.

She was a little worried by the thought that she was stealing the horse, but by now she

was fairly sure that the old woman and her son had taken the car, and she wondered if that made it all right to take something that belonged to them. She decided that it probably didn't and that she would have to bring the horse back again as soon as possible. 'I'll just borrow it,' she told herself.

The big brown dog had stayed close to her while she got the horse ready. Now, as she rode across the field, she was glad to see him trotting behind.

It was clear that the horse would not move fast, but he would not grow tired in a few hours as Janey would have done, and his feet would not get sore. Perched high on his back, Janey felt almost happy again. The sun was shining, the Germans had not come, and she was going home.

For the first two hours they met no one. They passed one field where a couple of men were working but otherwise the whole countryside seemed empty. All the life of it had drained away on to the roads.

It was not possible to avoid these roads completely. Some of them simply had to be crossed. The first time Janey came to a road crowded with refugees she thought for a moment that she had gone round in a circle, for it looked so exactly like the road she had left behind. But she checked the direction by the sun and made certain that this was a new road, cutting across the path which she had to take to get home.

She reined in the horse and sat for a moment watching the strange sight which had now grown so familiar to her—the slow-moving line of cars and farm carts, the women pushing prams, the tired trailing children, all of them running away from the Germans, all of them moving in the same direction.

It seemed to her, now that she was looking closely, that there were not so many cars as yesterday, more farm carts, more people walking. At first she was puzzled. Then she realised that the people with cars had been able to get away quicker. Also perhaps you could not get petrol any more.

As she crossed the road, squeezing through between an old man with a huge wheelbarrow and a boy on a wobbly bicycle, she heard a woman shouting 'You're going the wrong way, child! Don't you know the Germans are up there?'

When the sun was right overhead, Janey jumped down from the horse's back and sat under a tree while she ate another of her eggs and one of the apples. She was careful to choose a tree with a low branch which she could climb on to, so that she could mount the horse again from there.

All that morning the dog had trotted along behind her. Now he sat at her side, watching eagerly while she ate. She gave him a little piece of egg and then some of the chocolate, which he liked. She wondered whether he would be able to catch rabbits for himself later, if he got hungry enough.

It was not long after this that they came to another busy road, running roughly from north to south. On the far side were flat empty fields stretching for miles. In the field just opposite a fine crop of wheat was growing. Janey knew that the crops would probably never be harvested that year, and yet she did not like to trample them down. So she decided to cross the road and ride northwards until she came to the end of the growing wheat and could follow a track which ran eastwards between the fields.

This time she crossed the road behind a huge red truck which blew a puff of black smoke into her face. She shut her eyes for a moment while she coughed to get rid of it. When she stopped coughing and opened them again she heard the sound of aeroplane engines and, looking ahead of her, she saw three black dots in the sky.

Instantly there was panic everywhere. People leapt from the vehicles and tried to crawl under them, for the ditches were too shallow to give cover. Those who had nowhere to hide scrambled frantically into the fields. Women clutched their babies and screamed at their children.

Janey urged the horse into a trot and rode him through the wheat crop. Just as she did so, three German planes zoomed down low with their machine guns blazing. They came one after the other, straight along the line of the road.

Janey had never heard the sound of machine guns before. She never forgot it again for the rest of her life. It came back to her many times in dreams from which she woke sweating with fear.

She leaned low and clung to the horse's neck, but there was no need to urge him forward now. He put his ears back and raced over the fields faster than she would ever have believed that he could move. The trouble was to get him to stop, but he finally came to a halt on the edge of a small wood and stood there breathing hard and shivering.

Janey stroked his neck and whispered to him. She was shivering too and she found that she was gasping and sobbing. She tethered the horse, flung herself face downwards into the long grass, dug her

41

fingers into the earth and lay there until she was calm again.

When she sat up, she saw that the brown dog was not with them any more. This upset her badly, for she knew that a bullet might have struck him. She imagined him lying wounded on the roadway and she knew it was not possible to ride away. She began to walk back, whistling to him.

When she had gone about halfway towards the road she saw him. He was racing across the field towards her at top speed. He must have run very fast and very far when he heard the guns, and now he was in a state of great excitement. It took her several minutes to get him quiet again.

'All right, boy,' she said, as she stroked him and hugged him. 'It's all right, they've gone now. Quiet, now, quiet! They won't come back.' But as she spoke she was thinking, 'Won't they?'

From that time on, she knew that the dog would stay with her—that he was her dog now. The thought was comforting. She stroked his thick, rough coat and remembered the terrifying moment when she first saw him, with his big eyes gleaming like the eyes of a green monster in the light from the headlamps of the passing car. She decided to call him Ghost in memory of that first meeting.

They were all growing tired now. The horse plodded more slowly. Ghost did not leap around any more. But Janey was determined to travel farther.

They had to cross a main railway line and then another road with French soldiers travelling along it. Janey was very frightened while she was near the road, but no planes came.

As the sun sank low in the sky, they passed close to a little village with smoke coming from the chimneys of two of the cottages. Janey was tempted to stop and ask if they would take her in for the night but she had grown suspicious of unknown people. Instead of stopping, she tried to get the horse to move faster so as to leave the place behind as quickly as possible.

The next small cluster of houses looked better. There was no smoke and no sign of anyone moving around.

Janey watched for a little while from the other side of a field. Once more, the country was very bare here, with almost no trees. If she went to these houses she would have to ride up openly, so that anyone there could see her coming.

She wondered if she should sleep on the hillside instead, wrapped up in the blankets. The thought of sleeping out did not frighten her, now that she had Ghost to keep her company, but she needed more food, for herself and also for him. So far, he did not seem to be a great rabbit hunter.

She made up her mind suddenly and rode firmly across the field. No one appeared as she came near. Four cows were clustered by the gate of a farmyard, wanting to get in and be milked. From time to time they opened

43

their mouths and bellowed in pain. Hens were running around, but there were no horses. Janey supposed that the people had taken all the horses to pull the carts when they went away.

She climbed down and led her horse into the yard, managing to keep the cows out, though this was not easy. All the time she kept glancing around her and looking at the closed shutters on the windows. But everything was still.

She left the horse and walked down the lane at the side of the house. This led her into the village street—for there was only one street, with narrow red brick houses standing close along it. One bigger house lay farther back on the other side, with a wrought-iron gate and a wild looking, weedy garden. All the shutters on all the houses were closed.

Janey went very quietly along the street, almost on tiptoe. It was like being in an enchanted town, where some witch had put everyone to sleep by a wicked spell. Yet you could not know for certain whether anyone might be wakening from the spell behind those dead-looking shutters, watching you.

Janey was hoping to find a shop where there might be some food that Ghost could eat. But there did not seem to be a single shop in that tiny village—nothing but the silent houses and the silent church beyond them. She came back to the farmyard feeling that she hated this place.

She decided to milk one of the cows and

then sleep. In the end, she milked them all, although her eyelids kept closing with weariness and she had far more milk than she could use.

There was a barn with a great pile of hay in it. Janey made up her mind to sleep there, instead of trying to get into the house.

While she was milking the cows, Ghost had gone exploring. She whistled for him now and in a moment or two he came into the yard with something in his mouth. She went to look and saw that he had found a big hunk of meat which someone must have thrown out before leaving. She was very relieved, for that solved one problem meanwhile.

The horse was standing patiently in the yard. It was his turn now. Janey gave him water to drink and a big pile of hay to eat. He seemed contented.

It was growing dark so she brought the horse into the barn and tied him up. Then she whistled for Ghost, who had vanished once again. When he came back she spread a blanket out on the hay and he curled up and went to sleep beside her.

Chapter 5

The next morning was bright and sunny once again, like all the mornings of that month of May. It was now Sunday, the 19th.

Janey wakened quite late, for it was dark inside the barn and she had been very tired. She got up at once and went out into the farmyard, rubbing her eyes. She splashed her face with water from the pipe that stood in a corner of the yard and went to look for eggs. It was easy to find a dozen or so. The next thing was to light a fire and boil them. Once again it was easy, for there was a big pile of wood lying beside the barn. In no time the fire was blazing and crackling and the water in the little iron saucepan was beginning to boil. Janey was just about to put the eggs in when she heard a noise behind her.

She turned around sharply. A boy of fifteen or sixteen had come into the farmyard and was standing watching her. He was big and rough-looking. Janey noticed that he had huge hands. He grinned in a strange way, not friendly.

'Nice horse!' he said, pointing. 'I like that horse.' His voice sounded strange, too. There was something childish about it, as if he was much younger. And yet it was deep, like the voice of a man.

'You can't have the horse,' said Janey. 'It's mine.' As she spoke she realised that this was not quite true, and she blushed.

The boy grinned again and began to move towards her. Janey moved sideways, towards the horse. But she could not mount without something to climb on, and in any case she could not have got away, for he would just have grabbed the halter.

She grabbed it herself and backed away from him, taking the horse with her. The boy came after her, still grinning. And now he was holding his hands out in front of him, stretching his fingers wide, at the level of Janey's throat. Her mouth felt dry and her heart was pounding.

The barn was behind her. She dodged sideways, letting the horse go. But the boy ignored the horse and came towards her until he was only a yard or two away. Janey screamed. The boy's grin grew wider as if the scream pleased him. Then suddenly round the corner came a huge brown monster, teeth bared, snarling.

The boy's eyes widened, his hands dropped, the grin disappeared. Ghost looked twice his real size, for his thick hair was standing out all around him. The boy ran, with Ghost after him. As he scrambled over the fence, Ghost caught his jacket between his teeth, tearing a large ragged piece of it away.

Janey whistled then, and Ghost trotted

back with the piece of cloth still in his mouth. He dropped it at Janey's feet, looking very pleased with himself. She hugged him.

After that she wasted no more time. She did not think that the boy would come back but she wanted to get out of the village, just in case. At the same time she was determined not to go without the eggs now. She boiled them till they were hard and packed them in the canvas bag. Then she put out the fire carefully, checked the direction by the sun, and rode away.

Now Janey wanted to avoid other people even more than she had done before, and that morning she was lucky. She saw no one except when there were roads to cross, and even on the roads it seemed to be quieter. Over great stretches of that sunny countryside, bright with the leaves of May, there was no human being anywhere except a small girl on a big grey horse, riding home, with her dog trotting behind her.

Sometimes Janey heard planes in the distance and this made her very nervous, but they did not come near.

She stopped by a stream at lunch time, choosing a place where there was a big boulder so that she could use it to climb on the horse's back again. She had now given him a name. She had decided to call him Plodder because of his slow, steady, patient walk. Plodder drank thirstily at the stream.

They had travelled only a few miles beyond that place when Janey began to hear a noise coming from the east. It was a dull, crunching, thumping sort of noise that came for a while and died away and came again. At first she thought it was distant thunder, but it was not quite like thunder and there were no storm clouds in the sky. Ghost whimpered when he heard it and stayed close to Janey with his tail between his legs. Janey looked down at him, and then she looked up at the clear horizon where the dark sound was coming from. She drew in her breath. There was no doubt about it. It was the sound of guns.

Janey had just admitted to herself that the sound was gunfire when she came to the first real barrier on her path. She rode down by the edge of a wood and found herself suddenly on the banks of a canal with no bridge to be seen.

Janey looked down at the long green weeds which straggled out into the dirty green water, and she looked across at the steep concrete bank on the other side.

Plodder could not swim over there. If he went in he would never be able to get out again.

In a way, Janey was glad to see the canal. There were many canals near St Quentin and so it seemed to be a sign that she was travelling in the right direction and was coming near to home. But she had to find a bridge to cross.

As she hesitated, a long, rolling rumble came from the east, louder than before. Ghost whimpered again, put his ears back flatter than ever and ran a few yards along the path to the right before turning to look at her anxiously.

'All right,' said Janey. 'You've decided it, Ghost. That's the way we'll go.' She tugged at the reins and followed him. And in a way it was a good choice, for they did not have to travel far before a bridge came in sight. The only trouble was that there were soldiers on it.

For one bad moment, Janey thought they might be Germans. But she was soon certain that they were wearing the familiar uniform of the French army.

Even that was bad enough, for she did not want to talk to soldiers at all. She hesitated and almost turned back. But she was unwilling to waste time and decided that if the soldiers were French they would not do her any harm. She rode up to them.

There was a young officer, with five men holding rifles. The officer spoke to her.

'Where are you going, little one?' he asked.

'I am going back to my father,' Janey told him.

He patted Plodder's neck and looked up at her. He saw a soft, round face, very pale, with dark brown eyes that looked down at him firmly.

'Where is your father?' he asked her.

His voice was so kind and his face looked so friendly that she made a bad mistake and told him. At once the officer shook his head.

'You cannot go there, little one,' he said.

He spoke in a strong voice, as if there was to be no argument. Janey knew that it was an order. She gripped the reins more tightly.

'But I must,' she said. 'I have to find my father. I have to get home.'

'Not now,' said the officer. 'The Germans are in St Quentin and we are fighting them between there and here. You can't go through the battle lines.' Then he looked at her face again and he added: 'Later, when we have beaten them, you can go home.'

'But I have nowhere else to go now,' said Janey.

That turned out to be another mistake. The officer looked troubled, then called to one of his soldiers.

'Go with this child as far as the post at the end of the village, and put her on the next truck that's going to Compiègne. Surely someone will look after her there. It will be better than St Quentin anyway.'

The soldier saluted, took hold of Plodder's reins and led them across the bridge and down the road on the other side.

Janey was filled with rage. She knew that the officer was trying to help her. 'But he has no right to stop me!' she thought. 'He's just stronger than me, that's all.' She was so angry that she tried to kick the soldier's arm. 'Hey! Stop that!' he cried, and slapped her leg hard. She gave up and sat scowling at him.

The army post was in a little house built of red bricks, with yellow ones making a pattern above the windows. It was the last house in the village on the south side. As they arrived there, a small truck was getting ready to leave. The soldiers tried to lift Janey into it without Ghost, but she cried and kicked so hard that they gave in.

'Let the poor kid take her dog,' she heard one of them say.

'All right. Put them both in the back,' said another one.

So Janey and Ghost were dumped in the back with the canvas bag, while two soldiers climbed up in front beside the driver. Plodder was turned loose in a field by the roadside, since the soldiers had no use for him.

Janey sat in a state of cold fury. Ghost tried to lick her face. The truck gathered speed along a short straight bit of road, swung round a corner, then stopped with squealing brakes. Right across the road lay a much bigger truck, turned over on its side, and a huge farm wagon with its axle broken. They had crashed into one another a few minutes before. There was no way past them.

The soldiers leapt out at once from the front of Janey's truck and rushed to try to help. As soon as she saw what had happened, Janey leapt out of the back with Ghost behind her and ran as fast as the heavy bag would let her. She scrambled up a steep bank covered with long grass and wild flowers and crossed the first field. Then she turned north again, taking cover behind a line of trees.

It was not hard to find Plodder, for he was still grazing near the army post where the soldiers had left him. He had wandered some distance from the road and was munching the grass beside a single apple tree that grew all alone in the middle of the field.

Janey could not risk going over to him in case the soldiers would see her. She hid behind a bush and whistled to him but he took no notice, so she could only watch helplessly as he grazed quietly, moving nearer to her and then, maddeningly, farther away again.

After a while, this was nearly too much for her to bear. She had to keep telling herself not to spoil everything by going out to get him. 'You'll just have to wait till he comes near,' she said to herself sternly. 'And if he doesn't come near, you'll just have to wait all the hours till it gets dark and fetch him then.'

All this time Ghost lay quietly beside her with his nose between his paws, as if he understood why they were there. And the sun moved very slowly over the sky.

Once she had really made up her mind to wait, Janey began to think about other things. She thought about the things the officer had said to her. Was it true that the Germans were in St Quentin? And how would she get through the battle lines? She had very little idea of what battle lines would be like, but she remembered the sound of the guns. Though she listened hard she could not hear them now, only the bees among the clover and the drowsy sound of the grasshoppers from the meadow. Her eyelids began to close. Several times she forced them open to see where Plodder was, but each time they closed again more tightly. She let her head rest on Ghost's warm back and she fell asleep.

Chapter 6

Janey was wakened by a crunching sound right beside her. She jerked her head up, startled, and looked straight into Plodder's face. His mouth was full of grass and he was munching steadily with his big jaws. He had found her while she slept, and now he was grazing behind the bush, only a few feet away.

It was growing dark. Janey took the halter and they moved off silently.

She walked for almost a kilometre before she found a fence and managed to climb on to Plodder's back again. After that she rode for two more kilometres before she stopped for the night. She wanted to get well away from the army post but she did not want to travel far because she had no idea where she was now going. The sky was full of bright stars but she did not know enough to find the north-east by looking at them. She made up her mind that she would learn to do that as soon as she got the chance again.

There were no houses in sight. She fed herself and Ghost on eggs and chocolate again, and shared the rest of the milk with him. Then she curled up in a ditch, wrapped in her blankets, and fell asleep. Soon now she would be home.

When Janey awoke the next morning she listened at once for the guns, but the only sound she could hear was a lark singing far above her in the bright sky. She rode cautiously north-eastwards across calm sunlit fields, wondering when she would come to the battle lines.

She never did, for they were not there. The French officer had not told her the truth when he said there was fighting going on between his post and St Quentin. Perhaps he did not know the truth, for it was not easy to get news at that time. But the truth was that the Germans were not yet ready to attack towards the south, for they were too busy trying to drive the British army into the sea. And the French were no longer trying to force a way northwards.*

So Janey saw no more French soldiers as she rode on. But before noon that day she saw her first Germans. While she was crossing a field in the direction of an empty roadway, two motor-cycles with sidecars appeared from behind a low hill. There were three soldiers on each of them. They wore a different uniform—a grey one—and dif-

* The gunfire which Janey had heard the day before came from the town of Crécy on the river Serre where a French colonel called Charles de Gaulle was commanding an attack on the Germans. But the attack was defeated; and before the day was over the French soldiers were forced to withdraw to the south again.

ferent helmets. A machine gun was mounted on each sidecar and the soldiers carried rifles. Janey held her breath and pulled hard on the reins. There was nowhere to hide. One of the men glanced at her, but they roared past without stopping.

To Janey's terror, they were followed almost at once by three aeroplanes. She swung Plodder round and raced him back across the field. But the planes, too, swept past her harmlessly. A few minutes later she heard several loud bangs from the west where they had gone, and she saw flames and smoke against the sky.

Soon after that she crossed a railway and discovered another canal ahead. She was thankful to see a bridge a little way along on the left—and to find that it was empty. She rode across it, holding her breath in case there was a trap, with soldiers hiding somewhere. But no one jumped out to stop her. Around her, the fields lay still.

In spite of the sunlight, Janey shivered. Not even a rabbit bobbed its tail at her among the grass. Once again she remembered the kind of fairy story where all living things are held frozen in a strange spell. She shook herself, as if to make certain that she could still move, and rode slowly on.

That afternoon she came at last to a place that she recognized. There was a familiar clump of trees beside a familiar straight stretch of road that ran along a raised bank of earth, higher than the fields on both sides. Janey's heart gave a jump of joy, for she knew that home was not far away. She turned Plodder's head and set him to climb the bank, and as they reached the top of it she saw what she expected to see: the first sight of the great church of St Quentin, called the Basilica, rising out of the hazy mist on the horizon.

Janey was so happy at that moment that she stopped right in the middle of the road and sat there gazing. But the moment of joy did not last long. It was quickly ended by the sound of car engines, still distant, but coming nearer.

As soon as Janey had recognized the sound, she kicked hard at Plodder's flanks to urge him over the road and down the other side. In the field at the foot of the bank she found a French army truck, lying on its side. She leapt down and crouched behind the truck, holding on to Ghost, while a long convoy of German tanks and armoured cars rumbled past above the level of her head.

The French truck had been packed with crates and one of them had burst open. Janey did not really look at it, but Ghost did, or rather he sniffed at it, and the smell made him so excited that Janey could hardly hold him. She did not understand until she saw the end of a long salami sausage sticking out. She let him have it at once, and he was still chewing it when the sound of the German engines had died away.

Janey took three more of the sausages and stuffed them into the canvas bag. Then she headed for home.

Now all the places she passed were familiar to her and she knew exactly where to go. The house lay among fields over the brow of a little hill.

As she rode up the other side of the hill, the thought came to Janey that the house might not be there. The queer feeling of being in a strange enchanted world had vanished while she looked at the Basilica and hid from the Germans and smiled at Ghost's excitement over the sausages, but it was coming back again. You could take nothing for granted any more. The whole world might change.

So when she saw the walls of mild yellow brick among the trees where they had always been, her eyes filled with tears of joy.

Plodder had started to munch the grass, as he did whenever they stopped for a moment. Janey was tugging on the reins and kicking with her heels to get him to move again when she heard the sound of a car on the

road below and looked eagerly down to see if it was her father's. But the first glance told her that it was not. It was a big black open car, and in front of it there were two motorcycles, just like the ones she had seen earlier that day. Two more motorcycles came roaring along behind. Janey watched in horror as they all turned into the drive and swept up to the front door.

She could not see very clearly after that because of the trees, but it seemed to her that a soldier jumped down and held the car door open for another fatter soldier, who climbed out slowly and walked into the house. The motorcycles were taken to the back door. The car did not drive away.

Janey slid down from Plodder's back and lay in the grass, so that no one would see her while she watched and waited for the fat soldier to go away—and for a sight of her father. But she did not see her father, and the fat soldier did not come out again. Instead, two more cars drove up to the house, and more soldiers went inside and stayed there.

Hours passed. Plodder grazed near her. Ghost ran away and came back again. Evening shadows grew long.

With a sick feeling inside her, Janey began to try to face the truth. The Germans were living in the house. Her father was not there.

All the way home, Janey had kept a picture in her mind of how his face would look when she ran to meet him. Even when the officer had told her that the Germans were in St Quentin she had never admitted to herself that her father might have gone away.

But where was he? Had they captured him? Had they taken him away? What had they done with him?

These questions pounded in Janey's mind, and she looked down at the house with a black feeling in her which was a feeling of hate, although she did not give it a name. These men down there had come and taken *her* home to be *their* home. And where was her father?

She shook herself at last. There was no point in staying here all night. But where could she go? Then an idea came to her that she would go to the cottage where Marianne's mother lived. It was even possible that Marianne might be there, though Janey had no strength to hope any more.

The cottage was not far off—a few miles out in the country. She found it closed and silent, like so many of the others.

There was a small barn behind it. Janey crept in there and curled up. She was so miserable that she ate no supper. She lay and cried herself to sleep.

Chapter 7

Janey was wakened in the morning by the sound of Ghost whining at the barn door, asking to be let out. She rubbed her eyes, which were still sore and swollen, and the memory of yesterday came back to her like a dull pain. She got up slowly, peeped through a crack in the wood to be sure there were no Germans in sight, and let Ghost go.

He began to explore the yard eagerly, sniffing along the fence post and round the old water butt. Janey went back into the barn and sat down wretchedly on the hay.

She sat there for a long time, looking down at her feet, slowly running her fingers through her hair to pick out the bits of straw. She knew she should at least get breakfast for herself and the animals, but she felt more like crawling right to the back of the barn and staying there. She wished she could sleep again and shut out this day.

It was a spider crawling over her hand that made her leap up in the end and brush it off with a shudder and go outside. The sun had risen quite high and Ghost had vanished. Her lips were moving, ready to whistle for him, when she saw something that made her stop. One of the windows of the cottage was open. Janey was certain that it had been closed the night before.

For the second time that morning she went back into the barn. This time she closed the door quietly behind her. Then she peeped out through the crack again and waited.

As Janey watched, it seemed to her suddenly that all of this had happened to her before and that she knew what would come next—or at least that it would be quite familiar when it came. As soon as she had this thought, the curtain behind the window stirred and a leg appeared over the window-sill. It was a bare leg, not the leg of a soldier. A boy swung himself out into the yard.

He wore short leather trousers and sandals and a dark red shirt. He was about the same age as Janey, but tall and strong-looking, with thick fair hair. He turned round, leaned back into the room, and pulled a small sack over the sill.

Janey was furious. 'He's stealing things that belong to Marianne's mother,' she thought. And without taking time to ask herself whether it was a sensible thing to do, she rushed out into the yard.

'Thief!' she shouted. 'You're a thief!'

She shouted it in French, of course, for that was the language she had been using all the time during these last days.

The boy gave her one quick, suprised look, and then ran lightly away, taking the sack with him.

Janey was more angry than ever. She whistled for Ghost and looked hurriedly all round her to see if he was coming. But it was not Ghost who appeared from the other side of the barn. It was the boy!

Janey did not understand how he could possibly have got back there so quickly. She noticed that he did not have the sack with him any more. He stared at her as if he had never seen her before.

Then she heard Ghost barking from somewhere out in the field where the boy had gone when he first ran away. She went quickly across to the fence to see what was happening.

Ghost was standing at the foot of a tree and he was looking up into the branches with his hair all fuzzed out the way it went when he was angry. Janey wondered if he had seen a cat and chased it up there. She called him back, but he did not come.

Now the boy had come over to the fence beside her. Suddenly he shouted something in a language that Janey did not understand. She supposed it must be German. At once another voice answered in the same language. The voice came from the tree.

The boy listened and nodded. Then he raced back across the yard and picked up an old rusty piece of metal that was lying in the far corner. It was long and heavy, so that it made a dangerous weapon. He grabbed it firmly in his left hand, climbed over the fence, and began to move slowly across the field to the place where Ghost was standing.

Janey saw at once what he was planning and she knew that Ghost might be in real danger. She jumped over the fence too, ran as fast as she could towards the tree, put her arms tightly round the dog's neck and turned to face the boy. Ghost was growling.

'You're a nasty German!' Janey shouted. 'And you're a thief, too! But I won't let you hurt my dog.' This time she shouted it in English though she did not know why.

The boy stopped walking. She saw his cheeks go red.

'I am not German,' he said. 'You must never call me that again or I will have to kill you.' He spoke in English, to Janey's great surprise. It was correct English, but it sounded stiff and strange.

'But I heard you,' said Janey. 'I heard you speaking German. Don't tell lies.'

'That was not German,' said the boy. He lifted his head proudly. 'That was Polish,' he told her.

Then, looking up at the tree, he spoke in the same language again. By this time Janey had forgotten all about the voice that had come from the branches. She turned round just in time to see another pair of bare legs dangling below them. And then another boy stood on the grass beside her—another boy exactly the same as the first one.

Janey looked from one to the other and she started to laugh. The boys smiled politely, as if they were quite used to this.

'Now I see what happened,' said Janey. '*You* were the one who came out of the

window and Ghost chased you up the tree. Then *you* came round the other side of the house. I thought you were one German boy and you were really two Polish ones.'

She stopped laughing and looked at them seriously.

'But if you are really Polish,' she said, 'how did you get here? And how have you learned to speak English so well?'

'We'll tell you all about that,' one of the twins promised. 'But we should not stay out in the middle of the field in case the German soldiers see us.'

'Come back to the barn, then' said Janey. She was beginning to feel very hungry. 'Come back and have breakfast with me.'

The boys smiled again. 'We had first breakfast long ago,' one of them told her. 'But we'll have second breakfast with you if you like.'

'We always have two breakfasts in Poland,' they explained.

Their eyes widened when they saw the salami that Janey had found. She guessed that they were hungry and she told them they could eat as much as they liked, for she knew where to get more.

So they sat in the barn together and the boys told her how they had come all the long way from Poland to the fields of northern France.

Their names were Tadek and Stefek Pulaski. Their home was in a village far away in the High Tatra Mountains.

'They are very high,' said Stefek. 'Very high and very beautiful. There are no mountains like these anywhere else in the whole world.'

Their mother had been English. She had taken them to England once when they were very young but they could not remember it.

The German soldiers came into Poland with their tanks and their guns at the beginning of September, 1939. The twins' father was an officer in the Polish cavalry. He died charging against the tanks. Then the men of the Gestapo came and took their mother away. The boys did not know why they had taken her or where they had taken her. They did not know whether she was still alive.

The boys themselves had managed to hide. Later, one of their father's friends had helped them to get out of Poland, through Hungary and into Yugoslavia. In Yugoslavia they went to the seaport of Dubrovnic and stowed away on a ship that was sailing to Marseilles in the south of France. The captain found them after the first day, but he was kind to them. He even gave them some food and some French money and he helped them to slip ashore in Marseilles without being seen by the French police. Then they had started to travel north through France, walking for many miles, but riding on farm carts sometimes. It had taken them a long time.

'We were planning to go to England,' said Tadek. 'But the Germans came to France too before we could do that.'

'We are still planning to go there,' Stefek added. 'It will be harder now, but we will find a way. Then we'll look for our grandmother, who lives there. As soon as we are old enough we are going to join the British army and fight the Germans.'

'We won't even wait till we are old enough,' said his brother. 'We look older than we really are. We'll tell them we are about fifteen already. They can't prove it is not true, for they will not be able to get our birth certificates.'

Janey thought to herself that they did not look as old as that. Also she thought their grandmother would surely know their age, but she did not say so. Instead she began to tell them how she had been trying to get to England too, but how she had come back to look for her father and had found Germans in the house when at last she got home.

'Then I came here,' she explained, 'because this cottage belongs to Marianne's mother. And I found you taking things from it and got very angry.'

'I am sorry,' said Stefek. His cheeks had got red again. 'I am not a thief really. I shall put them back.'

'No,' said Janey. 'Marianne's mother would want you to keep them. I took things also from other houses. When I called you a thief I forgot that I had done exactly the same. We'll all give the things back when the war is over.' She looked at Plodder and grinned. 'I even took a horse,' she said.

'You'll have to leave *him* behind when we go to England, I'm afraid,' said Stefek, 'He would sink the boat!'

Tadek had finished his second breakfast and was running about the barn playing with Ghost. He stopped running and jumped on to the hay again, panting and laughing.

'We must move west now towards the coast,' said Stefek. 'Then we have to find a fisherman who will take us across the sea.'

But Janey shook her head. 'I can't come yet. I think my father will come back here. Or Marianne will come and bring me news of him. I want to wait. I don't want to go to England without knowing what happened to him.'

The boys were silent. They had had to leave Poland without knowing what happened to their mother. One of them said gently: 'If the Germans have taken him, you will not be able to find out what happened, Janey.'

Janey's eyes filled with tears. But she spoke firmly. 'Perhaps they have not taken him. I want to wait. You go to England. I'm staying here.'

The twins looked at one another. Then they both began to speak at once. 'We'll stay too,' they said. Stefek went on: 'This is what we'll do. We'll find a good hiding place near here and we'll stock it up with food from the place where you got the sausage. Then while we wait for your father we'll fight the Germans.'

'What do you mean?' Janey asked. 'How can we fight the Germans?'

'Oh, there are many ways,' Tadek told her, waving his arms about. 'We can cut telephone wires. They won't like that at all. And we can stop their trucks from running. We know a lot about engines. Our father taught us. He was in the cavalry but he knew everything about engines. There's a bit you can take out and then it won't start.'

'But the first thing is to find a good place to hide,' said Stefek. 'Janey, you know everywhere round here. Have you got any ideas?'

'Why not stay in this barn?' Janey suggested. 'Or in the cottage?'

Stefek shook his head. 'The Germans might easily decide to come round and look in all the houses,' he answered.

Janey thought again. 'I know an old quarry,' she told him. 'There are lots of big boulders in it and there are thick bushes growing. We could make a house by putting planks over two or three of the boulders, and then we could cover the planks with branches to make it look like bushes.'

'That's called camouflage,' said Tadek.

'That's better,' said Stefek. 'But there's usually only one way into a quarry and the very best hiding places have back doors.'

Janey looked thoughtful. 'Back doors ...' she repeated slowly. 'There's the old millhouse then. It's got a cellar and there are *three* ways into that cellar. There are two trapdoors in the floor, but there's another way also. You go up some stairs and out through a door in the back wall. And elderberry bushes grow all over that door now, so you would hardly know it was there, especially in summer. Nobody has used the mill for ages. It's a bit of a ruin so I was not supposed to go inside it. My father said it was dangerous.'

'Where is it?' Stefek asked her.

'Well, that's the only trouble,' she admitted. 'It's just two fields away from our house. And the Germans are in our house. But there are some thick trees in between,' she added.

'Sometimes it's good to hide near your enemies, where they don't expect you,' said Tadek.

Chapter 8

They left Plodder in the field beside the cottage and they went to see the millhouse.

It had a fine big cellar, dry and warm. There was a wooden ladder under one of the trapdoors and a chute under the other, for sliding bags down. The wood had begun to rot in places, so some of the rungs of the ladder were not strong. They checked them all carefully and remembered which ones they must never stand on.

The mill was built on a piece of sloping ground, lower towards the back where the mill stream flowed past and where the elderberry bushes grew on one side of the mill wheel, hiding the old doorway. Janey had been right. You could hardly see the door at all unless you parted the bushes and crawled through.

'It's a good hiding place,' said Stefek. They decided to move in.

That afternoon they began to fetch supplies of food from the overturned lorry. They brought biscuits and tins of meat (though they had nothing to open these with) and more salami sausages and sugar and coffee. They took Plodder along, and they filled some of the old sacks that they found in the mill and slung these over his back.

Several times they saw German trucks and motor cycles on the roads but these never stopped.

'They are not interested in us,' said Tadek. 'They think we are only children.'

'And they are quite right, too,' said Janey, grinning.

'Ah, but they do not know what we can do to them,' said Tadek. He scowled and looked as fierce as possible.

In the evening, Janey said she wanted to go out alone and watch the house.

'I just want to see what's happening there,' she said. 'And I want to do it myself.'

'Don't stay too long, then,' Stefek warned her. 'And don't get too close.'

Janey nodded. She slipped out by the back door and followed the mill stream until she came to a bend from which you could see the front door of the house.

There were small trees and bushes all along the edge of the stream, and at the bend there were one or two taller trees. Janey climbed into the branches of a young beech tree and sat there watching.

She could see the window of her own bedroom near the back of the side wall and she was very upset when she caught a glimpse of someone moving inside there. But everywhere else the house seemed to be still. Then she heard the noise of an engine purring along the road and in a minute the big black car with its motorcycle escort came into sight again, travelling from the direction of the town.

As the car turned into the driveway, Janey leaned forward to get a better look. But she leaned too far and lost her balance. With a great crackling of thin branches, she fell to the ground. Her ankle bent under her and she gave a gasp of pain. As she sat rubbing it, she heard a voice saying in French: 'Does it hurt very badly?'

She looked up quickly. A tall man was standing behind her, dressed in the grey uniform of the German army.

At first Janey saw only the uniform, she did not look at his face. A wave of fear hit her and in spite of the ankle she got up and tried to run. The man stopped her at once by catching hold of her shoulders. But he held her quite gently, not hurting her.

'Sit down,' he said. Janey sat on a stone,

with her heart pounding and her ankle throbbing.

The man felt carefully all around the ankle bone.

'It is not broken and I do not think it is badly sprained,' he said. He looked at Janey. Her blue dress was quite dirty now and her arms, sticking out of it, were very thin. Her face was white.

'Where do you live, child?' he asked her. Janey did not answer. Her fear of him was growing less but she certainly was not going to tell him where she lived.

He shook his head and sighed.

'Are you afraid of me?' he asked.

She nodded.

'I will not hurt you,' he told her quietly.

Then she spoke to him for the first time: 'Are you a German?'

'Yes,' he said, 'I am a German. Have they been telling you that all Germans are wicked and cruel?'

She nodded again.

'It is not true,' he said. 'Do not believe them.'

'How can you speak French so well?' she asked him then, as she began to feel braver.

'Because I was a teacher of French before I was in the army,' he answered. 'I used to teach French and English to German children.' He smiled. 'Most of them did not learn it very well,' he added.

Janey opened her mouth and then shut it again. She had been going to speak to him in English but she had decided that it would not

76

be wise. It would be better to pretend to be a French girl.

'What's wrong?' he wondered. 'What were you going to say?'

'Do you live in that house now?' Janey asked him in French.

'Yes, I do.'

'Do you know where the people who lived there before have gone?'

'No, I don't,' he said. Then he looked at her closely. 'Why do ask that? Do you know them?'

Janey did not answer. Instead she stood up, moving carefully, and told him: 'I have to go home.'

'I shall take you home if you will tell me where to go,' he said. 'I shall drive you there in a car.'

But she shook her head. 'Thank you. My ankle is better. I can walk now.'

She limped slowly and painfully across the field, not going in the direction of the mill.

The tall German officer watched her for a few minutes. Then he crossed the stream by the stepping stones and went towards the house.

At the door he met his friend Josef. 'It is sad, Josef,' he said. 'Out there just now I met a waif of a child and she was terrified of me.'

'How can you be surprised, Karl?' said Josef. 'That is what war is like.'

'But there was something odd about the child,' Karl added, as they went in to dinner together. 'And she was very interested in this house. I think she was watching it.'

'A spy, then?' said Josef, laughing a little.

Karl was just about to answer him when the General came into the room. The officers clicked their heels together, and the General sat down at the head of the table, in Janey's father's chair. Lieutenant Karl Werner sat down in Janey's chair beside him. They ate a very good dinner and drank several bottles of Janey's father's wine.

Chapter 9

Lieutenant Werner was interested in the countryside. He liked to study wild flowers and to watch birds and butterflies. Whenever he was not on duty he went for walks, taking his field glasses with him.

Soldiers do not usually have much time for peaceful walks in the country when they are fighting in a terrible war, but during those days there was a short time of quietness around St Quentin. Most of the fighting had moved farther to the west. It was part of Lieutenant Werner's job to get ready for the next German attack towards the south, but that attack was not going to begin until June. Meanwhile he was sometimes able to have an hour or two when he could try to forget about the war.

On Wednesday, the 22nd of May, there was to be a meeting in the town hall of St Quentin. Some senior German officers were coming to begin to make plans for the new attack towards the south and the great city of Paris. But the meeting was not to take place until later in the day.

Lieutenant Werner decided to get up very early and go for a walk. He headed northwards, striding over the fields with his long legs, tossing his head back and whistling. But soon the whistling faded away.

It was always the same on these walks. After a time they made him feel sad. He found it very strange to walk for miles and to see no people. The empty cottages and fields troubled him deeply. He thought about the people from these cottages who were now far away from home, trailing along strange roadways, tired and hungry and frightened, wondering when the next planes would swoop down to bomb them; and he knew that he hated war. But he was caught up in it now. There was no way out of it except by becoming a deserter from the army and that seemed impossible to him. He told himself that he was doing his duty for his country.

He sat down on the edge of a clump of trees and took out his field glasses to look for birds. A wide silent valley lay below him. The waters of a small river made a gleaming silver line across the green fields. He swept his glasses slowly along its banks. Hardly a bird was moving. 'Have they gone with the people?' he wondered sadly.

He had put down the glasses and was scanning the whole valley without them, when a flash of red drew his eyes to a small farm about a hundred yards across the river. At once he lifted the glasses again and looked closely. It was a boy with a red shirt on. He was moving in the farmyard.

Lieutenant Werner felt a surge of pleasure. Perhaps the farmer and his family had come home. He followed the boy's movements, watched him put something in a sack, and saw him disappear into the barn.

The lieutenant went on watching, waiting for him to come out again. Then a very strange thing happened. The boy who had gone into the barn came out through one of the farmhouse windows!

Lieutenant Werner let the field glasses fall and rubbed his eyes. He was sure the boy had gone into the barn!

For a moment he had the wild idea that there was an underground passage between the barn and the house. But who ever heard of a tiny farmhouse with a secret passage? Somehow he must have failed to see the boy when he crossed back over the yard. Yet he knew he had been watching all the time.

He raised his glasses again and he began to laugh. For now there were two boys in the yard, two boys exactly alike.

'Twins!' he muttered to himself. 'Of course! Twins!'

He watched what the twins were doing and he stopped laughing.

'They are stealing things,' he thought. 'They are looting that farm.'

His first notion was to run down the hill and try to catch them. Then he stopped himself.

'Poor children,' he thought. 'If they have been left all alone because of the war, what are they to do? They have to try to live somehow.'

But he was puzzled when he watched to see

what the boys were taking. It was hard to make this out clearly, but it didn't look like food, more like tools.

'Perhaps they are trying to build something,' he thought. 'Maybe they have nowhere to live and they are building themselves a little hut.'

He watched as the boys climbed on to the back of a big grey farm horse and rode away. Then he followed, keeping at a good distance up the slope.

They went the same way that he would have to go to get home, but before they reached the house they turned south-eastwards. He saw them cross a bridge over the stream that flowed past the house, and then turn right towards an old building that had once been a mill. He had noticed the place before and had thought that it might be interesting to go and take a look at it some day.

The boys vanished from his sight and did not appear again on the other side of the building. But in a few minutes a small, dark-haired girl, wearing a blue dress, came out from behind the mill leading the grey farm horse. She turned the horse loose in the field.

Lieutenant Werner noticed that the girl was limping a little. He looked at his watch. It was time to go in and report for duty.

While Lieutenant Werner was reporting for duty to his General, the twins were stacking the tools in a corner of the cellar. They had come back with a fine collection of weapons: hammers, spanners, knives, saws, wire-cutters and pliers. Janey added her hatchet to the pile. 'That will be useful too,' said one of the boys. Janey thought it was Stefek, but she was not quite sure, for they looked very much alike and they spoke in exactly the same way. But she had noticed that Tadek was more excitable. He jumped about more and waved his arms in the air. Also he was left-handed and Stefek was right-handed, so you could sometimes tell in that way.

The twins had found long trousers for themselves and a dress for Janey. The dress was made of brown wool. She was glad to have it, for now she could wash the blue one, which was very dirty. The new dress was too big, but that didn't matter.

'Now,' said Stefek, 'the next thing is to decide where to attack.'

But first they held a council of war in the cellar around a flickering candle.

'We shall call ourselves the Young Eagles,' said Stefek. 'We must each promise now to fight the Germans with all our strength.'

And he knelt down in front of the candle and said: 'I promise to fight the Germans with all my strength for the honour of my country.' At once Tadek did the same. Janey was not quite sure what it meant to fight for the honour of your country and she hesitated. But she did not want to be left out of the Young Eagles, so she knelt down and said it too.

That afternoon they went to choose their first target.

Janey insisted that her ankle was much better now and that she was going to show the twins the shortest way into the centre of the town. For this expedition they left Plodder behind, but they took Ghost with them in case he would bark when he was left alone. He had no collar but they put a piece of rope around his neck, loosely tied.

On the way into town they passed a large yard outside a factory building. 'It's some kind of engineering place,' said Janey. There were six German trucks in the yard and they saw another one drive in. They crossed over to the other side of the street so as not to go too near the sentry who was guarding the gate. The yard had railings all round it, but there seemed to be only one gate and only one sentry.

'We could get over these railings in the dark,' said Tadek. 'It would be easy.'

The centre of St Quentin was full of German soldiers, as they had expected. The children were very nervous at first, but the soldiers took no notice of them. There were a few other people on the streets as well but they all hurried along quickly and did not stop to speak to one another. Janey saw no one that she knew.

They passed only two shops that were open. One was selling freshly made bread that smelt good, so they bought two long loaves with Janey's money. It seemed very strange to be in a shop again getting food in an ordinary kind of way. Janey discovered that the twins could speak hardly any French at all.

They reached the town hall and stood for a moment watching. It was clear that something was going on. German soldiers kept going in and out. The sentries at the door kept leaping to attention as officers passed them.

'I expect they keep records in there to show where all their tanks and things are,' said Janey.

'Yes,' said Tadek, 'and they probably have maps on the walls with flags stuck in to let them see how far they have advanced.'

Stefek nodded. 'That must be the headquarters. We must cut the telephone wires to that building. And perhaps we could even get inside and tear up some of the maps and papers.'

They were just going to cross the street to see where the wires entered the building when two German motorcycles swept past them, followed almost at once by a big black car. The roof of the car was down and Janey could clearly see the tall German officer sitting in the back beside another older man with a fat red face. She looked away quickly, but Lieutenant Karl Werner had seen her too, and he had seen the boys with her. He said nothing about them to the man who was with him. The two officers got out and walked under the stone archways into the town hall.

Chapter 10

The German sentries outside the town hall of St Quentin were feeling hot in their heavy uniform. The sun beat down steadily on their steel helmets. It was four in the afternoon and the bells in the old tower above their heads began to play their funny cracked tune.

One of the sentries swore. 'That din hurts my ears,' he said crossly. 'We've taken this place. It's ours now. Why can't we stop the noise?' He was feeling bad-tempered because of the heat and because he was thirsty. When the bells began to play he had been thinking what it would be like to put his lips to a long, cold glass of beer.

The other sentry just grinned. He was not really listening, for he was thinking of home. It was his daughter's birthday—the 23rd of May—and she was ten years old. He wondered whether she would be eleven before he saw her again—if he ever saw her again. Then he blinked. A little girl was coming across the square towards him with a taller, fair-haired boy walking by her side.

For just a moment the sentry thought that the girl was his daughter and his heart jumped. Then he sighed as he saw that this child was smaller than his Eva. Her dark brown dress was too big for her, and the legs and arms that stuck out from it were very thin. She was carrying a big basket over one arm, with green leaves laid on top. The boy had another one, just the same.

The children came to the edge of the pavement and hesitated. The girl looked up at the sentries and they saw her large dark eyes in her small pale face glancing timidly from one of them to the other.

The sentry who had a daughter of his own asked her what she wanted. He asked it in German, because he did not know how to speak French. She still hesitated, and he guessed that she did not understand him. So he walked slowly towards her.

As he came close, the child pulled back the green leaves from her basket, showing him that it was full of the most beautiful ripe strawberries, freshly picked. Then she lifted her hand and pointed to the inside of the building.

The sentry smiled. Now he understood why the children had come, and it pleased him. He shouted to his friend: 'They have come to sell strawberries to us. That is good. These little ones are not so foolish as to run away. I shall take them inside to the kitchen, Hans. Fresh strawberries! Think of that!'

Hans made a noise in his throat that was a kind of growl. 'Fresh strawberries for the officers, I'll bet. Not for us!' But he took two or three from the basket which the little girl held out to him as she passed. 'Better hurry back,' he said to Gustav. 'The Captain won't like it if he sees that you're away.'

'He'll be as pleased as anyone to have the strawberries,' said Gustav. But he came back very quickly, for he knew that Hans was right.

Ten minutes later the two sentries saw the little girl and the fair-haired boy walking into the square again from the side of the building, with empty baskets over their arms.

'Must have come out by the back door,' said Gustav. Hans nodded. By this time he was feeling too thirsty to speak. The children waved to the sentries and went away.

No one saw the little girl and the fair-haired boy when they crept towards the town hall again at midnight. They came by a different way this time, from the side of the building.

Two new sentries had replaced Hans and Gustav at the front door. At the back, a tall railing enclosed a little yard. Two other sentries were posted at the gate of this yard, facing the square which had been the fruit market before the Germans came. But they stood there chatting to one another, relaxed and careless, for they were expecting no trouble. They were the conquerors. What was there to fear?

At the side of the building, the windows at ground level had iron bars on them. And the windows on the floor above were too high to reach. But at the corner, where the railing joined the wall, it was possible to climb up.

One of the children crept out from the shadows and tossed a small stone against the window that was nearest to the top of the railing. Then he darted back again and held his breath in case the sentries would turn their heads. But they were too busy grumbling to one another about being left behind in this dull town while their comrades raced on with General Guderian to drive the British army into the sea.

In a few seconds the window above the railing was opened very softly from inside. Then two dark shadows, one after the other, began to climb up towards it. The first one had already slipped into the building and the second one was nearly at the top of the railing when one of the sentries suddenly stopped speaking in the middle of a sentence. 'Ssh! What's that?' he said urgently.

The child on the railing did not hear the words but he saw how the sentries stiffened their bodies and raised their heads. He stopped moving and clung there, where he was, with his heart pounding in his chest.

'Where?' said the other sentry, looking vaguely from side to side. 'What is it?'

'Over there!' said the first one, pointing across the market place. 'I thought I saw something moving in the shadows.'

'Better go and look, then,' said his comrade. 'Just to be sure.'

So the first sentry moved quickly away across the square, and the other one leaned forward, watching closely while behind them the child on the railing slipped through the window, closing it gently behind him.

In the room inside, the fair-haired boy who had opened the window grinned in the darkness. You could see very little except the flash of his white teeth.

'Did you see that?' his brother whispered. 'I thought they were going to look round.'

'But they didn't,' said Stefek. 'I think we are in luck tonight.'

'How did you get on?' Janey whispered to him.

'Fine!' he said softly, and he grinned again. 'It was easy. I hid in a cupboard under the stairs when you went out and I stayed there till everything was silent. The only thing I was afraid of was that they might lock the cupboard, but it only had brooms in it so there wasn't much risk. Then I crept out and came here, as we planned. How about you?'

'Fine too,' said Janey. 'Tadek was waiting for me round the side after I went out by the back door. Then we walked to the front again and waved to the sentries so they'd be sure to see us.'

Tadek chuckled. 'So they saw one boy going in and they saw one boy going away again and they never guessed that one was still inside.'

'So it worked well,' said Stefek. 'But now we have a lot of work to do. Come on! Don't waste time.'

Stefek had gone scouting around a bit before the others came, so he already had a good idea of where they should go. He was fairly sure that there were only two men on duty inside the building. They were in a room on the ground floor and he thought they were looking after the telephone switchboard. He had seen them going in there as he peeped through a crack in his cupboard door. You could see a line of light under the door of the telephone room now, and you could hear their voices sometimes. But in the rest of the building everything was quiet.

The Young Eagles were very busy for more than an hour. They had two small torches with them, and some tools. The windows of the main offices were hung with heavy dark curtains, so there was not much risk that the light from the torches would be seen outside.

No one disturbed them as they worked. The Germans seemed to be very sure that the building was safe. After all, most of the French people had gone away, there were no French soldiers close by, and the Germans were certainly not expecting to have their headquarters attacked by three small children.

When the work was done, the Young Eagles left silently by the way they had come. As they tiptoed past the telephone room they heard the two men laughing.

Tadek grinned. 'They are going to have a nice quiet night in there now,' he whispered.

The last child to leave the building closed the window gently behind him. The sentries did not hear a sound.

Chapter 11

Sergeant Friedrich Hochberg was a very keen soldier. He liked being in the army and he was proud of doing his job well. He had been put in charge of the offices in the headquarters at St Quentin under the supervision of his captain.

It is true that Sergeant Hochberg would rather have been fighting, but he knew that a soldier must do whatever he is told to do and that his job was important. He was specially pleased when meetings were held at the town hall and generals came to make plans and everything ran smoothly because of him. He got very angry if something went wrong.

There had been a meeting on Wednesday and things had gone well. All the papers and maps had been ready, the telephone operators had been efficient, and whenever the officers had asked for information they had been given it at once. Afterwards the captain had congratulated him.

Now it was Friday, and there was to be another meeting today. Sergeant Hochberg knew that the reason for all these meetings was that plans were being made for a new attack. He also knew that the Führer himself had to be told about everything that was happening.*

'Perhaps one day the Führer himself will come to a meeting here,' the sergeant thought, and his heart beat faster at the idea. He hurried into the office early, to see that everything was in order.

The first place to visit was the telephone room, to find out what news had come in during the night. The night operators had to wait until he arrived before going off duty.

'Right,' said the sergeant briskly. 'Let me see the messages.'

The two soldiers looked rather puzzled.

'It was a very quiet night, sergeant,' one of them told him. 'Nothing at all after midnight.'

'Nothing at all?' said the sergeant sharply. 'No reports of troop movements? No reports of bombings? No one asking for supplies? I don't believe it!'

He looked at them suspiciously. 'Did you leave your post?' he roared suddenly.

They both jumped to attention, looking terrified. 'No, sergeant!' they said. 'Not for a moment,' one of them added.

'For your sake I hope that's true,' Sergeant Hochberg told them. 'Well, get me our office at Abbeville *now*. I need to know what's happening over there—and I need to know it fast!'

---

* Führer is a German word which means 'leader'. This is what the German people called Adolf Hitler.

One of the soldiers turned instantly to the switchboard while the sergeant began to pace up and down the room. But he had not taken more than a few strides when the soldier spoke again, in an anxious voice: 'Sergeant, the phones seem to be dead. I can't get a line.'

Sergeant Hochberg's face got very red and the veins stood out on his forehead.

'What?' he yelled. Then almost at once: 'You there! Fetch a technician. Quick!'

While they were waiting for a technician, Sergeant Hochberg went upstairs to the office where the records were kept. There was a filing cabinet for the less important papers and a safe for the secret ones. The key to the filing cabinet was kept hanging on a board inside a small box on the wall, along with the keys of other doors and cupboards in the building. Sergeant Hochberg and the captain were the only people who had keys to the safe and to the box where the other keys were kept. The sergeant was very proud of this.

He went first to get the key to the filing cabinet, thinking as he did so about the telephones. He was really worried about them. He took his bunch of keys from his pocket in an absentminded sort of way and started to fit one of them into the keyhole of the box on the wall. Then his jaw dropped and his eyes widened. The box had been forced open—and it was empty.

His roar of anger brought an orderly running from the conference room next door. The man had been cleaning the room and he still held a duster in his hand. He could do nothing to explain what had happened but it helped sergeant Hochberg to have someone to shout at.

The orderly was thankful when the door of the room opened and one of the telephone operators appeared. He had been running up the stairs and he was out of breath.

'Sergeant,' he gasped, 'the telephone wire was cut!'

'So!' said the sergeant grimly. 'There is no doubt that it's sabotage then. Well, I'll deal with it, I promise you that! Someone will suffer for it. Is the wire fixed?

'The man's doing it now,' the operator told him.

'Right! Get Abbeville the moment it's working.'

And, taking the bunch of keys from his own pocket, Sergeant Hochberg carefully picked the right one for the safe.

It went in as it ought to do, but it refused to turn. There was something inside the keyhole jamming it. Sergeant Hochberg kicked the safe so hard that he hurt his toes in spite of his heavy army boots. Then he ran down the stairs into the telephone room. 'Get a locksmith,' he cried. 'Phone for one!'

The telephone operator turned pale. 'But sergeant,' he said, 'it's not working yet.'

'Why not?' shouted the sergeant. 'How long does it take that fool to join two bits of wire together?'

'Not just two bits, sergeant,' the soldier told him. 'The technician mended the first break we found, but the lines were still dead. So then we started to check all the wires inside the building. They had been cut in twenty-three places!'

'When I catch the man who did that, he'll wish he had never been born,' said Sergeant Hochberg.

Then he jumped at the sound of a cool voice speaking just behind his left ear.

'What is the crime that will bring this terrible punishment?' it asked. Sergeant Hochberg swung round and saluted smartly. The captain had walked into the room.

The captain's voice was not cool any more when he had heard the story. He snapped out orders angrily, with his dark brows pulled down and his thin lips held in a hard line. The meeting was less than an hour away.

At this moment a motorcycle drew up in the square outside and a soldier rushed in and saluted. 'From Colonel Ebbinghaus, sir,' he said. 'An urgent message to be sent to Charleville—for the Führer himself, sir!'

'It will just have to go by radio then—coded of course,' said the captain. 'Take it at once to Lieutenant Müller. Tell him to deal with it personally.' And he handed the message to one of the telephone operators, who saluted and hurried away.

As he was leaving, the operator almost bumped into the sergeant, who was hustling a rather small, odd-looking soldier through the door. The soldier's nose had been broken in a fight long ago and was badly bent. He also had huge ears. His mates called him 'Segelohren' which means 'Sail-ears'. It was an affectionate nickname, for they all liked him.

'This man is a locksmith, sir,' said the sergeant, clicking his heels together.

It was not quite true. Segelohren did know a great deal about locks, but he did not usually tell people how he had found out. The truth was that he had been a burglar before the war and he had been very good at his trade. They took him up to the main office.

Segelohren fiddled with the locks of the filing cabinet and the safe for a few minutes. Then he shook his head so that the great pink ears wobbled a little.

'I think it's sand that's in there, sir,' he said. 'Very difficult. Nothing you can do. Need an oxyacetylene torch, sir.'

The captain ground his teeth together. 'Have you got an oxyacetylene torch, sergeant?' he asked in a tight voice.

Sergeant Hochberg looked very unhappy. 'Er ... no, sir. Not right here, sir,' he answered.

'Then why didn't you think of bringing one, you fool?' cried the captain, losing his temper at last. 'Get an oxyacetylene torch at once!'

'An oxyacetylene torch?' said another voice, very surprised. 'What's going on here? The place is like a madhouse.'

The colonel had arrived.

The captain barely had time to tell him what was going on before the door opened again. This time it was Lieutenant Müller. He was a tall, stiff-looking man who did not usually show his feelings. But now he was not managing to hide them.

'Sir,' he said to the colonel, 'I apologise for this interruption, sir.' Then, turning to the captain: I have to report, sir, that I am unable to carry out your orders. The valves of the radio transmitter have been smashed. Someone appears to have hit them with a hammer.'

The captain controlled himself with great difficulty. He looked at the colonel. 'You see, sir,' he said, 'it is serious. Someone did a great deal of damage here last night. We cannot know yet if it was a traitor among our own men or an enemy agent who got into the building.'

'It should not have been possible for anyone to get into the building,' said the colonel coldly. 'You should have seen to that, captain.'

Now it was the captain's turn to look unhappy. But before he could reply, the sound of motorcycle and car engines filled the room. The colonel crossed quickly to the window. One of the generals was driving into the square.

Chapter 12

Afterwards it was Lieutenant Karl Werner who was given the job of finding out what had happened.

He had never been a detective before, but he did his best. He began by checking every window in the town hall to see if any of them had been forced open from the outside. He could discover no evidence of this; but he found one window which was shut but not locked.

He sat down and thought about this window for a while. So far as he could see, three things were possible. The first was that someone had forgotten to lock the window and that an enemy agent had just been very lucky and had found it. Lieutenant Werner did not think that this was at all likely. The second possible thing was that an enemy agent had been in the building earlier in the day and had unlocked the window so that he could easily climb back in at night. The third possible thing was that the agent had got into the building earlier in the day and had stayed there in some hiding place until night came. Then he had climbed out by that window but had not been able to lock it again behind him.

Lieutenant Werner knew it was possible

that the enemy agent was really a German soldier—a traitor. But it was also possible that he was a Frenchman. So the first thing was to find out if any Frenchman had been in the building the day before.

The lieutenant sent for the men who had been on guard duty during the day and he questioned them. They all told him that no Frenchman had passed through the doors.

'Are you quite sure?' he asked them. 'Think now! Is there anyone you might have forgotten?'

But they all shook their heads, and he had to admit that it was not likely that they would all have forgotten.

The last one that came was a big fellow with a Bavarian accent. He was more talkative than the others.

'No Frenchmen came here, sir,' he said, 'The place is dead and the ones who are still around keep away from us as if we smelt bad or something. That's why I was so pleased to see the children. They weren't afraid of us.'

'The children?' said Lieutenant Werner, leaning forward in his chair. 'What children?'

'The ones who brought the strawberries, sir—the baskets of lovely fresh strawberries.'

'Tell me about the children who brought the strawberries,' said Lieutenant Werner slowly.

'Well, sir, there was a little boy and a little girl ...'

'One little boy?' asked the lieutenant, interrupting him.

'Yes, sir. One little fair-haired boy and a little dark-haired girl. About nine or ten years old, sir, I'd say. I have a girl of ten myself, sir, you see, and she ...'

'Stick to the point, man,' said the lieutenant. 'What happened when these children came here?'

'Well, we let them in, sir,' said the soldier.

'But you told me that no one went in except Germans,' said the lieutenant.

'No, sir,' the guard answered. 'Beg your pardon, sir, but you asked me if any Frenchmen went in. You didn't ask me about a couple of kids.'

The lieutenant sighed. 'You are quite right,' he admitted. 'I should have thought more carefully about that question. Now, did you let these children wander around inside the building on their own?'

'No, sir, certainly not, sir. I took them straight to the kitchen.'

Lieutenant Werner sent for the cook. The cook remembered the children well. They had gone out by the back door. The cook admitted that he had not gone right to the back door with them, because he was busy. But he had shown them the way.

Lieutenant Werner sent for one of the men who had been on guard at the back door.

'Do you remember seeing two children leaving the building?' he asked.

The man thought about it for a moment. 'I remember seeing one child, sir,' he said. 'A little girl with two empty baskets.'

'With *two* baskets?' the lieutenant asked him.

'Yes, sir. I think so, sir.'

The other guard from the back door agreed that there had been one child. He could not remember how many baskets.

Lieutenant Werner sent for the front door guards again.

'Did you think of checking to see if both these children had left the building?' he asked them.

'Yes, sir. They did, sir,' said one of the men.

'But they went out by the back door, so how do you know?' said the lieutenant.

'Because they came through the square again. They waved to us. We saw them.'

'Both of them?' the lieutenant insisted.

'Both of them, sir,' they told him firmly.

Lieutenant Werner sent them all away and sat there for a long time, thinking.

He was sure now that he understood what had happened. The problem was what to do about it. His duty as a soldier was clear enough: he should send in a report saying that he suspected it was the children who had caused the damage at headquarters. He should also say that he thought he knew where they lived.

But what would happen then? First of all the children would certainly be captured. After that they would probably be handed over to the Gestapo.* Lieutenant Werner

* The Gestapo were the secret state police. Everyone feared them.

realised that the Gestapo would be sure to wonder if the children were part of some organization, and if there were men who were training them and telling them what to do. So they would try to make the children tell them who these men were. If the children said there were no men, the Gestapo would just try all the harder to make them talk. Lieutenant Werner was a kind man, and he did not like to think about that. He realised that he had a grave problem.

At the end of the afternoon, Lieutenant Werner went to see the colonel and told him that he had not yet finished his inquiries. But he said he was now sure that no Frenchman had been allowed to enter the building during the day before the sabotage took place.

'Does that mean you think it was the work of a traitor?' the colonel asked him.

'Not necessarily, sir,' said the lieutenant.

'Then what *do* you think?' asked the colonel in a very impatient voice.

'It is not an easy problem, sir,' said the lieutenant. 'I need more time.' And this was certainly true.

At dinner that evening he ate with a very poor appetite, though the cook had made a delicious meal for the general and his staff.

After dinner the other officers sat drinking coffee and brandy—Janey's father's best brandy. But Lieutenant Werner asked the general to forgive him if he did not join them that evening. He wanted to walk through the fields and think.

There were heavy clouds gathering in the sky as if a storm was coming. It seemed to Lieutenant Werner as if the weather was a perfect match for the state of his mind.

He wandered over to the stream and stood under the tree at the place where he had first met Janey. He remembered her small face twisted in pain because of the ankle. And he remembered the fear in her eyes when she saw his uniform.

'She would have good reason to look like that if the Gestapo got her,' he muttered.

Suddenly he made up his mind. He swung round and began to stride firmly along the river bank towards the mill. He had never gone really close to it before. From the other side of the stream he could see the elderberry bushes growing thick along the lower wall beside the old wheel. The place seemed to be in quite a good state of repair, he decided— probably fairly snug and warm and dry.

He crossed the bridge and turned back towards the building. The door opened easily on creaking hinges. As he went inside, a dog began to bark loudly.

Lieutenant Werner stopped at once, expecting the dog to leap at him, then realised that the sound was coming from underneath the floor.

'So there's a cellar,' he muttered. He looked around him. There was just enough light left for him to see.

At first he could not find any way to get down into the cellar. Then he moved some old sacks that were lying on the floor and discovered a trap-door which opened at once when he tugged at it. He peered down into the darkness.

The dog was now barking more loudly than ever. It sounded like a large animal and Lieutenant Werner found that he did not particularly want to go down there. He called out in French: 'Are you there, little girl? It's me. It's the man you met when you hurt your ankle. I won't hurt you!' But there was no sound except the fierce barking that went on and on.

Now that his eyes were used to the darkness, Lieutenant Werner could just make out the shape of the animal leaping about at the foot of the ladder. It was a long ladder, for the cellar was deep. He hesitated. If he went down a few rungs and crouched so that his head was below the level of the floor, then he could strike a match and see whether the children were there. He reckoned that the dog would not be able to jump high enough to reach him. He had a pistol in his belt but he did not want to hurt the animal if he could help it.

He put his foot on the first rung and began to climb down. But he did not take enough care. He was too worried about the dog to think of any danger from the ladder. The third rung was rotten and it gave way beneath the weight of his left foot. His right foot was already in the air, groping for the fourth rung, and just at that moment Ghost took a mighty leap upwards and caught his right trouser leg. Ghost might not be much good at catching rabbits, but he was a champion jumper. The lieutenant crashed to the ground, hit his head on the stone floor and lay still.

Ghost stopped barking immediately. He sniffed at the lieutenant's face for a moment. Then he lay down quietly beside him, with his nose between his big paws.

Chapter 13

The young Eagles had gone on another
expedition. They had left the mill only ten
minutes before Lieutenant Werner arrived.
This time the target for attack was the yard
where the trucks were parked.

Earlier in the day they had walked past the
yard and they had been delighted to see that
many more trucks were now there. The
trucks were being assembled for the attack
that was soon to come, though the children
did not know this.

The clouds that darkened the sky were
helpful to the raiders, and there was no
moon that night. They glided like shifting
shadows through the empty streets of the
town.

Each of the twins was carrying a length of
rope. The plan was to lasso a spike on the
railings. One of the children would then
climb up with the second rope and fix that to
the next spike, letting it hang down on the
other side. Then they could pass quickly over
the top, one after the other.

To do this, they needed darkness. So they
were dismayed to find, when they reached
the yard, that a searchlight was now sweep-

ing over it, with a long probing beam.

The searchlight had been fixed on the top of the factory building. They timed the sweep of it. It took three minutes to swing right across the yard and back again.

Three minutes was not enough time to fix the ropes and get three children over. The Young Eagles crouched together in the shadow of a side street and looked at one another.

'I don't think that searchlight was there this morning,' Janey whispered. The others agreed. 'They must have put it up this afternoon,' said Stefek. 'Perhaps they are taking more care because of what we did to their headquarters.'

The problem now was to work out another plan. No one wanted to give up and go home.

'Could we squeeze through?' Janey wondered. The boys did not think so, but they decided to try, for no one had a better idea. Watching the searchlight carefully, they raced from the street to the end of the factory building and crouched in dark shadow once again.

The obvious place to try was the gap between the end of the factory building and the first of the railings. When the beam of light was moving away towards the other side of the yard, Tadek did his best to squeeze through.

'If your head goes through, the rest of you will go too,' he said.

But Tadek's head was too big. And of

course Stefek's was exactly the same size.

'I'll try it,' said Janey.

'But you can't go alone!' The twins both spoke at once.

'Why not?' said Janey. 'It's not any more dangerous.'

'You don't know what bit to take out of the engine,' Tadek pointed out.

Janey had to admit that this was true. 'But I can let the air out of all the tyres,' she said. 'And I can take the valves away with me so that it won't be easy to blow the tyres up again.'

Stefek still tried to stop her, but Janey had made up her mind. She said: 'I promised to fight the Germans with all my strength, didn't I? Do you want me to break my promise just because your heads are too big?

It did not seem to be a very good reason for breaking a promise. Stefek gave in. 'We'll wait for you here,' he said. 'Take these pliers with you. You might need them to get the valves unscrewed.'

Janey put the pliers in her pocket and waited till the searchlight had begun to sweep over the yard away from her. Then she crept out from the shadow and put her head into the gap between the wall and the first of the railings. It was just small enough to get through! She wriggled the rest of her thin little body after it. By the time the searchlight came back, she was hidden under the nearest truck unscrewing the first of the valves.

Most of the valves would have been too

tight for her to turn with her bare fingers but she could move nearly all of them when she used the pliers. It was very satisfying to hear the hiss of air and to watch the huge fat tyres sinking to the ground and to think how angry the Germans would be in the morning. 'They won't be able to send this one away full of soldiers to fight against us,' she thought, as she stuffed valves into her pocket.

The twins watched her anxiously from the shadow of the wall. 'What if they notice that the tyres are going flat one by one?' Tadek whispered suddenly. None of them had thought of this.

'They'll be looking for people moving about. They won't be looking at the tyres,' Stefek replied. But they both began to feel very troubled.

'I wish she'd stop and come back,' said Tadek.

But Janey had no intention of stopping until all the trucks were done. As she worked, she found herself thinking all the time about her father. She had now decided that he was probably fighting with the British army, trying to get back to St Quentin and drive the Germans out. So every time a tyre went flat she felt that she was helping him.

She found it easy at first to avoid the beam of the searchlight. She just watched it carefully from the shadow of the truck she had dealt with and then darted across to the next truck in the darkness that followed its passage.

There were two main groups of trucks and between these there was a wider space. But she calculated that she would have plenty of time to get over it. She chose the moment carefully and ran.

She had not gone more than half way when suddenly the searchlight changed direction and began to swing rapidly towards her. She froze for a moment, then turned and raced back the way she had come. But she could not beat the searchlight. The beam caught her and dazed her and held her as she struggled to dodge away. She rolled under a truck, and the beam settled round that truck like a trap closing.

She heard loud voices and heavy feet. Then, in the brilliant light, she saw the huge leather boots of the German soldiers all around her. A long arm reached for her. She backed away. But the only result was that she came close enough for another long arm to

reach her from the other side. She was dragged roughly into the light.

From outside the railings, the twins watched in horror.

'What can we do, Stefek?' Tadek whispered frantically. Stefek just shook his head.

'I'm going in there,' said Tadek. 'I'm going to let them take me prisoner too!'

'Don't be a fool, Tadek,' said his brother sharply. 'It is your duty to stay free and go on fighting. Besides, we must stay free so that we can rescue her. We must try to see where they take her.'

But the soldiers bundled Janey into a fast car and drove her away. There was no hope that the boys could follow it. They went miserably back to the mill.

Chapter 14

Lieutenant Werner groaned and tried to open his eyes. It was difficult. The lids were too heavy. He gave that up and tried to move his legs but something seemed to be holding his ankles together. He tried his arms. Oddly enough, they seemed to have got twisted painfully behind his back, and something was holding the wrists together. He could not think what it might be. He tried his eyes again.

This time they opened but they would not focus properly. He could see blurred circles of dim light, spreading out and running into one another. He shook his head and felt a stab of fierce pain. He closed his eyes again.

The third time he opened them it was a little better. Instead of the muddled circles of light he could see a fairly steady candle flame. The candle was in the neck of a bottle and the bottle was on the top of a wooden box.

There was something else on the box also—something much bigger. And there was something dangling over the edge ... it looked like a pair of legs, not very large—boy's legs.

Lieutenant Werner made a great effort. He forced his eyes wide open and turned his head upwards. He saw a boy's face looking down at him. It was a handsome face, rather broad at the forehead, with a wide mouth and a straight nose. The candle lit it from the side. He could not really see the eyes.

He said in French: 'You must be one of the twins.' The boy did not answer, but another voice spoke, from somewhere behind the lieutenant's back.

The lieutenant could not understand a single word, but he realised that the language which the voice was speaking was either Russian or Polish; for these two languages are very much alike and he knew the way they sound, even though he did not understand them.

He tried to speak to the boys again, in German this time. The one on the box scowled at him and said: 'Schweinhund!' But the lieutenant did not think the boy had been able to understand.

The only other language which Lieutenant Werner could speak was English. He did not expect the boys to understand this either, but it seemed worth trying.

'Where is the little girl?' he asked. This produced immediate and dramatic results. The boy jumped off the box, waved his arms about and shook his fist in the lieutenant's face. 'You dirty German soldiers have her … they have taken her prisoner. Schweinhund!' he shouted. That was the only German word which Tadek knew.

The lieutenant groaned. His head hurt badly. He wanted to rub the sore bit gently with his hand, but his arms were tied behind his back. He tried to think. How had the little girl been captured, while the twins were still here? Certainly the Gestapo had not found this hiding place, for they would have left someone to watch it.

'What happened?' he asked. 'How did they get her?'

'Do you think we are going to tell you?' said the voice that came from behind him.

'If you do, I might be able to help you,' the lieutenant answered.

'Help us?' The boy's voice was scornful. 'First, we do not take help from Germans. And second, how can you help anyone when you are tied up and lying on the floor? You are not very strong now, are you? You are our prisoner.'

Lieutenant Werner was silent for a few moments. The boys spoke to one another in Russian—or Polish, whichever it was.

The lieutenant had not thought very clearly about what he was saying when he offered help. And yet now, when he did think about that little girl in a Gestapo prison, he knew that he wanted very much to help to rescue her. He also knew that he would probably be shot for doing it, if anyone found out, for the Gestapo would say he was a traitor. 'And after all they would be right,' he thought. Then he managed to smile at himself. It was absurd to be worrying about what he should do when he couldn't do anything at all. The boy was right. He was their prisoner.

'What are you going to do with me?' he asked.

The boy picked up something from the box beside him and the lieutenant was alarmed to see that it was his own *9mm* Luger automatic pistol. The boy cocked the pistol, released the safety catch, and pointed it at the lieutenant's head.

'We have not decided yet,' he said. 'We think perhaps we ought to shoot you.'

The lieutenant did his best to make his voice sound cool and firm.

'It is wrong to shoot prisoners-of-war,' he said. 'You must know that.'

Even in the candlelight you could see that the boy's face grew red. He spoke in a voice so low that the words were hard to hear: 'It is wrong to take mothers away from their children, so they do not know what happened, or anything.'

The lieutenant was silent again. Inside he was thinking: 'So that is what happened to them! Poor children! They must be Polish.' For one of his friends had told him that some bad things had been done when Poland was occupied.

'How did you and your brother come to France?' he asked gently after a moment or two.

The boy jumped off the box and stood looking down at him fiercely, with the pistol in his hand.

'How do you know I have a brother? You

have seen only me. What do you know about us? Speak, or I will kill you!'

'You have a twin brother,' said the lieutenant. He watched the boy's eyes widening in surprise. 'I know many things about you. I saw the two of you looting a farmhouse. I was watching through my field glasses. You were taking tools. I wondered why. I followed you and saw that you came back here. Then I saw the little girl bringing the horse out into the field. I had met her before when she hurt her ankle. Later I saw all three of you outside the town hall. And I know it was you who broke in there.'

As the lieutenant finished speaking, Stefek came and stood beside his brother.

'Since you knew all this, why did you come here alone?' he asked. 'Why did you not bring your men to capture us? Or did you think you could capture us all by yourself since we are only children?' He tossed his head back, and looked very fierce and proud.

'I did not come to capture you,' Lieutenant Werner explained. 'I came to talk to you. I wanted to tell you that you must not do things like that, for it is much too dangerous and you are sure to be caught in the end. And I was right, you see. For you tell me that the little girl has been caught already.'

'We shall rescue her,' Tadek told him.

The lieutenant began to shake his head, then stopped because it hurt too much.

'You cannot rescue her by yourselves,' he said. 'It is impossible. I don't suppose you even know where they have taken her.'

He watched the twins' faces and saw that he was right. Suddenly he made up his mind.

'Look,' he said, 'let me go and I shall help you. I think I can guess where they have taken her. I shall try to get them to set her free. If they will not, then I shall tell you where she is. I promise you.'

The twins looked at one another. Then they looked at him and they shook their heads.

'It is impossible,' one of them said.

'We do not trust you,' the other one added.

The lieutenant tried again.

'Listen, I do not know what time it is, because it is so dark in here. But if I am not back by breakfast time they will start to search for me and they will certainly reach this building before ...'

He stopped speaking in the middle of the sentence. Ghost had begun to growl and the hair on his neck was rising.

Chapter 15

'They may be coming already,' said the lieutenant in a whisper.

'You must hide—over there in that dark corner behind the boxes—no, inside them if possible.'

He paused and listened. He could just hear voices now, shouting to one another in German.

'Cut these ropes!' he said urgently. 'Quick, you young idiots! If they find me tied up they will search everywhere for the person who did it. And put that candle out! Hide it somewhere!'

The voices grew louder. So did Ghost's growl.

'If he barks there is no hope,' said the lieutenant. 'Keep him quiet if you have to strangle him! Now, *cut these ropes*!'

Stefek took his knife and cut the ropes. The lieutenant stood up stiffly and rubbed his head. They could hear more voices, then heavy feet outside.

'My pistol,' said the lieutenant, putting out his hand.

Stefek was holding Ghost now, keeping the dog's mouth shut with difficulty. Tadek shook his head. 'We keep the pistol,' he said.

'Give it to him, Tadek!' Stefek whispered in Polish. 'He's right. You may spoil everything.'

Very unwillingly, Tadek handed the Luger over. 'Everything is spoiled already,' he muttered. 'We are taking help from a German.'

The lieutenant put the pistol in his holster and began to climb the ladder.

As he did so he whispered: 'I'll meet you in two days at the farmhouse where you found the tools. I'll come early in the morning if I can.'

'Watch the fifth rung,' Stefek told him.

The heavy feet seemed to be close to the mill door now. The lieutenant realised that he must get the trapdoor open before the men came in or he could not say that he had just fallen down it by accident. If the trapdoor was shut it would be obvious that someone else had been there to shut it.

He had about five seconds to spare. His head was barely through when the mill door swung open and Captain Duncker walked in. Six soldiers carrying submachine guns stood behind him.

'Huh!' said the captain. 'Werner! There you are!'

Lieutenant Werner climbed out, clicked his heels and tried to salute. It was only then that he realised that his cap was not on his head. It must still by lying on the cellar floor. If the captain sent one of the men down to look for it …

'Sorry, sir!' he said feebly.

'Where's your cap?' said the captain. 'What happened to you, man?'

'I fell down, sir,' the lieutenant told him, feeling very foolish. 'I must have hit my head on the floor. It knocked me out, I suppose. I woke up a few minutes ago.'

'But what were you doing here, Werner?' the captain asked him.

'Just taking a look at the place, sir,' said Lieutenant Werner. 'I came for a walk after dinner. It seemed to be an interesting old building. I've always been interested in old mills—the machinery, you know.'

Captain Duncker frowned. 'Lieutenant Werner,' he said, 'allow me to point out that you are a soldier, not a tourist. Do not forget it.'

He turned to one of his men. 'Fetch the lieutenant's cap,' he ordered. 'And take care you don't fall down.'

As the soldier jumped to obey, the lieutenant cursed himself for a careless fool.

The soldier's head vanished below the floorboards. A moment later there came a crash and a yell which sent the captain rushing over to shine his torch down into the darkness. The man was sitting on the ground with a bewildered look on his face. The fifth rung from the bottom had given way.

'Idiot!' shouted the captain. 'Get on with it!'

The soldier picked himself up and looked around. There was the officer's cap, lying on the floor. He bent to get it. Close beside it there was something else—a piece of broken biscuit! He picked the biscuit up, sniffed at it, and crumbled it between his fingers. It was quite fresh! He shouted up to his captain:

'Something funny down here, sir!'

The captain moved back at once to the trapdoor.

'What is it?'

'Looks as if somebody's been living here, sir—and not long ago.'

'Right!' said the captain grimly. 'We're coming down.'

They began to search the cellar thoroughly. In a moment the crates of food were discovered, then the heap of tools. The captain himself found a candle in a bottle lying behind a box. He touched it with his foot and it rolled over. If he had picked it up he would have felt that the wax was soft and warm.

'Look everywhere,' he told his men, 'in every box and barrel. There might be a store of guns and ammunition.'

The beams of the torches struck into the corners lighting up the dust and the cobwebs as the spiders raced away.

One of the men found a canvas bag and handed it to the captain. He opened it and pulled out a bit of cloth—some blue cotton stuff—then a notebook with hard blue covers—no, a passport! A British passport! He looked inside.

Meanwhile Lieutenant Werner was watching as the men came to the last pile of boxes in the far corner. Three of them were over there, reaching inside, kicking the boxes over. He held his breath. What if the dog made a sudden grab for one of those searching hands? But why had no one heard the dog growling by now? Could those boys really have strangled him to keep him quiet?

'Empty, sir!' a man shouted. 'Nothing but dust in any of them!'

Lieutenant Werner could hardly believe his ears. How could two big boys and a huge dog vanish into the air?

Chapter 16

Colonel Koffka sat comfortably behind his big desk in a large chair while Lieutenant Werner stood uncomfortably on the other side of the desk, facing him. Between them lay a piece of blue cotton cloth, rather crumpled and dirty-looking, and a British passport.

The colonel spoke. 'Lieutenant Werner,' he said, 'I hear you had an accident last night. You fell into the cellar of an old building. Is that correct?'

'Yes, sir,' said the lieutenant.

'They also tell me that someone had been living in that cellar not long ago,' the colonel went on. 'These things were found.' He lifted the piece of blue cloth and held it up. It was a girl's dress. He laid that down, picked up the passport and opened it. 'Jane Elizabeth Longman,' he read. 'Born on the 16th of April, 1930.'

He put the passport down again and looked at Lieutenant Werner. 'A child of ten. An English child,' he said.

'English!' said Lieutenant Werner in a very surprised voice.

'You are surprised that the passport

belongs to an English child, but not that it belongs to a child,' said the colonel. 'Why not?'

Lieutenant Werner gulped. He realised that he would have to take more care.

'Werner,' said the colonel, 'You had better take care how you answer me. Had you ever been to that old mill before?'

'No, sir,' the lieutenant answered at once. He was very thankful to be able to tell the truth.

'Did you know that the child was living there?'

'Well, sir,' said the lieutenant, 'I wondered. I had met her—one evening when I was out walking. She was wearing that blue dress. She had hurt her ankle so I offered to drive her home, but she would not tell me where she lived. She seemed to be afraid of me.'

'You spoke to her, yet you did not know she was English?'

'No, sir. We spoke in French. As far as I could tell, she spoke it perfectly.'

'Hmmm,' said the colonel thoughtfully. He looked out of the window towards the north-west. That was where the fighting was now, over near Dunkirk, where they were driving the English soldiers into the sea. He wished he was there, for he would have liked to see that. But he had heard a strange story. It seemed that on Friday morning, quite unexpectedly, the Führer himself had ordered the German tanks to stop. He had ordered the tanks not to attack, just at the time when they could easily have won a complete victory. That was a very puzzling thing.

Yet the colonel still wished he was at Dunkirk, not stuck in St Quentin trying to sort out this kind of mess. Why was young Werner looking so uncomfortable? Did he just feel that he had made an ass of himself or was there something more?

'Werner,' said the colonel, 'you were given the job of finding out who was responsible for the sabotage in the town hall. You have not yet told me what you discovered.'

He watched Werner closely. The man looked more uncomfortable than ever.

'I have no firm proof of anything, sir,' Werner told him.

'But what do you *think*?' said the colonel.

'I would like to ask the little girl some questions before I answer that, sir,' said the lieutenant. He had decided that this was the best way to make sure he would discover where Janey was and get a chance to see her.

'That is, if we can find her, sir,' he added quickly.

'Oh, I think we can find her,' said the colonel. 'We found her last night, as a matter of fact. Do you know what she was doing when we found her?'

'No, sir,' said the lieutenant. Once again he was glad he could speak the truth.

'She was letting the air out of the tyres on our trucks,' the colonel told him.

'What?' cried the lieutenant.

The colonel thought to himself: 'Well, he

certainly didn't know that!' Aloud, he said: 'Yes. So it seems likely that she had something to do with the town hall sabotage also—as you suspected, I think. Well, if you want to ask her some questions I don't see why not. But the Gestapo men are holding her now. We shall have to arrange it with them.'

The colonel did not like the Gestapo men. He knew that they would not want one of his men to see their prisoner. This was enough to make the colonel think it was a good idea.

'Thank you, sir,' said Lieutenant Werner.

'You may go now, Werner,' said the colonel. The lieutenant clicked his heels, saluted and turned towards the door. But as he went the colonel called his name again.

'Sir?' said Werner, turning back.

'I think you had better watch how you behave in this affair,' the colonel told him.

Chapter 17

Janey heard the door shutting and the key turning in the lock. The men's footsteps faded away and she was left alone in the darkness and the silence.

She was lying on a stone floor where they had thrown her down. It felt cold against her arms and legs, it smelt damp and musty in her nose. She pulled herself into a little tight ball, and sobbed, and lay still.

Then, as she lay there, she thought she heard something. What was it? Her body stiffened and she raised her head an inch or two to listen. A tiny scratching noise! A rat? She got on to her knees and crouched there, staring around her into the darkness.

The noise did not come again, so after a little while she relaxed. As her eyes got used to the dark, she saw that she was in a fairly large room, but it seemed to have only two small windows, high up on one wall. Through these windows she could see a few little stars in the night sky.

She did not know where she was. The men had put something over her head in the car, so that she could see nothing. They had driven for a bit and then waited while someone got out and went somewhere and came back. Then they had driven again till they brought her to this place—but not far, they had not taken her far.

The noise came again—a little scuffling noise. If it was a rat, what would she do? She stood up quickly and clenched her teeth so as not to scream. Would it come close? Would it try to bite her? She looked around for a weapon, but the room seemed to be quite bare. She realised that there was not a table or chair or a lamp or a rug—not a bit of furniture of any kind, nothing she could climb on.

The noise stopped and it seemed to her that the sky was growing lighter. She thought about the twins. Had they got away? The stars meant that the clouds must have cleared.

She imagined what it would be like if the door opened and Stefek or Tadek was shoved in. She knew that she ought to feel very sorry if that happened, but she could only think how good it would be to see them again. Then she wondered where Ghost would go if they were all captured. Maybe she would never be able to find him again.

At this thought she began to cry. She did not dare to lie down in case a rat came, so she stood in the middle of the floor with tears pouring down her cheeks until there was enough daylight for her to see that the room was quite empty. No rat was there. When she was sure of this, she went over to one corner and sat down, resting her back against the wall.

She was exhausted by now, but she was too frightened to sleep. She thought that the men would come back for her and she did not know what would happen then. But, as the hours passed, she stopped being afraid that they would come and she began to be afraid that they would not come—that no one would ever come again.

The sun shone through the clouds and the beam of its light moved slowly, slowly, along the wall. Janey was very hungry and thirsty by now. Her mouth was dry, her stomach was so empty that it hurt, and her head began to feel funny. The sunlight shone on her in the corner and moved on. She shut her eyes, and at last she came close to falling asleep. But just as she was beginning to slide down into dreams, the key turned and the door was pushed open, so that it crashed back against the wall. Janey jumped and blinked and struggled to sit up and look at the two men who strode in.

She had only time to notice that they were not dressed like soldiers before one of them grabbed her right arm and jerked her on to her feet. Then the other one seized her left arm and they led her out of the door without speaking to her. They passed along a corridor, up a short narrow flight of stairs, along another corridor, through a wide hall and into a big bright room.

The room was furnished in a pleasant, comfortable way. There were pictures on the walls, and there was a thick blue carpet. A large bowl filled with roses stood on the grand piano. A large man with a big pale face was sitting in an armchair near the window. Beyond him you could see a rose garden, and clipped hedges and tall trees.

Janey was taken across the room until she stood in front of him. He looked at her silently for a moment, and then he spoke to her in French. It was not good French but she could understand it.

'What is your name?' he asked.

'Jeanne,' Janey told him.

'And your other name?' he asked again.

Janey did not know what to say. She did not want him to know she was English. 'Maupas,' she said, giving the name of a friend of hers at school.

The big man said something in German and the man who was holding Janey's right arm tightened his grip until it hurt, and slapped her face hard. She jumped and cried out.

'Do not lie to us!' the big man shouted at her, in English this time. Then he sat back and looked at her very angrily; but he spoke more quietly.

'I know your name,' he said. 'I have asked you that question to see if you would speak me the truth. But you have not. You must, or it will be very bad for you. Do you understand?'

Janey nodded and bit her lip. She was trembling.

'Your name is Jane Elizabeth Longman,' he went on. 'You are English. Why are you now in France?'

'I live here,' said Janey.

'Then where are your parents?' the man asked.

'My mother is dead. I do not know where my father is,' Janey told him.

He leaned forward. 'Why do you not know?' he asked.

Janey started to explain how she had been sent away, how the car had broken down, how she had come home. But as she spoke the man's face began to look funny. It started to move about in a kind of mist. She tried to make it stay still but it would not. Before she could finish the story, Janey fainted.

When she opened her eyes again she was lying on a sofa. The man who had been asking her questions was sitting on a chair a few feet away. The other two men had disappeared.

'I think you are hungry and thirsty, no?' he said to her.

Janey nodded. The man smiled, trying to look kind but not managing it very well.

'Soon we bring food and drink,' he said. 'But first you will tell me one thing. Who

sent you to escape the air from the tyres?
Now, speak me the truth, little girl!'

'No one sent me,' said Janey with an
effort.

The man frowned. 'I do not believe you,'
he told her. 'Little girls do not things like
that by themselves. We know that someone
sent you and we shall discover. Was it your
father?' He bent closer and peered at her.

'No!' said Janey. 'My father would never
send me to do a thing like that. I told you. I
don't know where he is!' She shut her eyes
again. 'I wish I did,' she murmured. Then a
thought came to her and her eyes jerked
open. 'How did you know my name?' she
cried. 'Have you captured my father? What
have you done with him?'

'Hah!' said the big man. 'So! You want to
know that, eh? But I will tell you only when
you tell me. Who sent you?'

'No one sent me,' said Janey weakly. 'It is
true.'

The big man was beginning to look puzzled. He got up and walked over to the window, where he stood for a moment with his
hands clasped behind him. Then he swung
around and came back.

'Who was living with you at the mill?' he
snapped suddenly.

Janey shut her eyes quickly and hoped that
he had not seen the look of surprise in them.
So they knew about the mill! Had they
captured the twins, then? If she said no one
was there, and they knew it was a lie ...

'Answer me!' the man roared.

'My dog!' cried Janey, raising her head from the sofa. 'Did you find my dog? Did you hurt him? Where's my dog?'

The man said one or two words in German in a very angry voice. Janey guessed that he was swearing. For a moment she thought that he was going to hit her but instead he turned and marched out of the room.

Janey let her head fall back again on to the cushion. They wouldn't bother about a dog, would they? But the twins—that was another matter. Janey felt almost sure now that the twins were still free.

The big man with the pale face charged across the hall and into the room on the other side of it, where Lieutenant Werner was waiting. Werner got to his feet, noticing the man's scowl.

'It's a hopeless business trying to get sense out of that child,' said the man angrily. 'If you want to try, you're welcome.'

'I'd like to,' Werner told him quietly.

'Over there, then,' said the man. 'Off you go!'

At the door of the drawing room Werner hesitated. 'You must be careful,' he was telling himself. 'They probably have a microphone hidden somewhere, or someone watching through a tiny peephole. That's the kind of thing they do.'

He turned the handle and went into the room. The child was lying on the sofa with her eyes shut, looking very pale and thin. 'How small she is,' he thought, as he looked down. She opened her eyelids, and he saw at once that she recognized him.

'We have met before,' he said. 'You remember?' But she did not speak to him.

He sat down close beside her. 'Is your ankle better?' he asked. Her head barely moved. Suddenly he was worried. 'What have they done to her?' he thought.

'Are you all right?' he asked urgently.

'I am so thirsty,' she told him. 'And hungry.'

The lieutenant felt anger raging in him.

'Have they given you nothing to eat or drink?' he asked. She shook her head.

'I'll be back,' said the lieutenant, and he strode away across the hall. The Gestapo man was still in the other room. Werner tried to hide his anger and speak calmly. 'I can get nothing out of that child until she has had food and drink,' he said. 'She is too weak to answer me.'

The Gestapo man shrugged his shoulders. 'Perhaps you are right,' he said. 'I usually find it works better when they are feeling weak, but we'll try it your way.' He reached out and rang a bell. Then he smiled. 'It will not be hard to make her hungry again if you fail,' he added.

A man came, answering the bell.

'Take soup and bread and coffee to our young prisoner,' the Gestapo chief told him. 'She is our first prisoner here,' he added, smiling at Werner again. 'It is a distinction.'

Werner went back to the drawing room and sat beside Janey. 'They are bringing food and coffee,' he told her. And in a few minutes the food came.

Werner helped her to sit up and he watched while she ate and drank. Then he carried the tray to a table and came back beside her again.

'Now,' he said, 'that's better, isn't it?' He smiled at her. 'I want to help you,' he went on. 'But you must talk to me a little or I cannot help you. The soldiers caught you while you were letting air out of the tyres of our trucks. Why were you doing that?'

'You came here to attack us,' said Janey. 'Why should I not attack you?'

Werner sighed. What could you say in answer to that?

'You do not understand about war,' he said, feeling helpless and thinking to himself that he did not understand about it either. 'You must not attack us, for you will just be caught, and that is not nice, is it?'

Janey looked scornful, but said nothing.

'It was you who broke into the town hall and cut the wires, was it not?' Werner asked her.

'Yes,' said Janey.

'How did you get in?' said the lieutenant. He felt he had to ask this but as he spoke he was praying that she would have enough sense not to mention the twins.

'I took strawberries to sell them,' said Janey. 'They let me in. It was easy to open a window. At night I came back and climbed in. It was easy.'

The lieutenant thought: 'Of course she has enough sense!'

Aloud he said: 'Jane, this is very important. Was there a man who sent you to do these things?'

'I will tell you that if you will tell me something,' said Janey.

'What?' asked the lieutenant, looking puzzled.

'How do you know my name?'

'Ah!' he said. He looked straight at her. 'If I tell you that, will you promise to tell me the truth?'

'Yes,' said Janey. 'I promise.'

The lieutenant thought to himself: 'I hope they are listening to this.' Then he told her how the passport had been found at the mill. Janey sighed with relief. So they had not discovered her name by capturing her father—and he might still be free.

'Now,' said the lieutenant, 'you must tell me the truth, as you promised.' And he asked once again his carefully worded question: 'Was there a man who sent you to do these things?'

And Janey answered, 'No.'

Chapter 18

'Here he is,' Tadek whispered. 'Already!'

Long before dawn the twins had climbed a tree to watch for the lieutenant coming. They were high up among its branches so that when the full daylight came they would be able to see a long way in every direction. For the question was: would the lieutenant come alone? But there was still only the pale grey half-light that comes before the sun has

risen, and a white mist lay on the meadows. Lieutenant Werner's tall figure came striding out of that mist suddenly, close to the farmhouse building. And who could tell what was hidden in the mist behind him?

Lieutenant Werner looked all around him. Then he whistled softly. A blackbird began to sing loudly in the tree above the twins' heads as if it was answering him. The twins stayed very still, scarcely breathing.

The lieutenant moved over and looked in the barn. Then he peered into the house through the window with the broken shutter. They heard him say something in a low voice. When he called again more loudly they could make out the words: 'Are you there?'

The twins looked at one another. Stefek shook his head. It was too dangerous to go down. There might be German soldiers quite near, waiting for a signal to close in.

Lieutenant Werner was standing now by the barn door. They saw him take a piece of paper from his pocket. He stood holding it in his hand for a moment, looking around him once again as if hesitating. Then he fixed it quickly to the door.

As he did so an aeroplane roared across the sky from the east. Lieutenant Werner gave a little jump and looked up at it—straight towards the tree. And the first rays of true sunlight began to stream out from the horizon, so that the twins' heads showed dark against the brightening sky.

Lieutenant Werner strode quickly across

the farmyard. 'There you are then!' he said in a cross voice. 'Young fools! Why did you not come down?'

'Why do you think?' asked Tadek. 'We are not fools. That is why we did not come down. How do we know you do not have other soldiers waiting near here to capture us?'

The lieutenant sighed and rubbed his brow.

'Listen,' he said, 'for there is not much time. They are sending me away—over to the west, where the fighting is. I am to leave this morning, in about an hour from now. So this is my last chance to help you.'

He paused. The twins sat silently in the tree, coldly distrusting him. The mist was still heavy on the fields. You could hear a car engine now in the distance. The lieutenant began to speak again.

'Do you see that paper on the door? It is a map. It will show you the place where Jane is being kept. Perhaps I am foolish to give you this information, for I am sure you will try to rescue her and then they will capture you also. But I promised you—so I keep my promise.'

Now Stefek leaned forward eagerly. 'Have you seen her?' he asked.

'I have seen her. She is all right—at least so far. And she is a brave little girl.'

'We know that!' said Tadek proudly, throwing back his head.

'What will they do with her?' Stefek asked.

The lieutenant drew in his lips a little. 'I

cannot tell you,' he said slowly, 'for I do not really know. I do not think they know themselves what to do.' Then, changing the tone of his voice, he said briskly: 'I have kept my word to you. Now I must go.' And he swung round on his heel and began to walk away. But after a few steps he stopped and looked back. 'If you do manage to save her, give up fighting the whole of the German army after that, will you?' They saw him smile at them and wave and disappear.

When he had gone there was a long silence in the tree. Even the blackbird had stopped its singing. The twins watched while the morning mist was slowly dried up by the hot sun. As it rolled away it let them see the empty, peaceful fields around them.

At last they slid down the trunk and ran across to the barn door. The map was clearly drawn and the distances were marked. The house where Janey was being kept prisoner appeared to be only five kilometres from the farm.

On the back of the map the lieutenant had written a message in capital letters: 'They are sending me away, so there is nothing more I can do. They have not really harmed her.'

Stefek put the map carefully into his pocket. 'Come on,' he said, 'let's get out of here.'

The boys had been living for the past two days in the old quarry that Janey had first suggested for a hiding place. They had built a kind of shelter by putting planks over some of the big boulders and covering the planks with branches and leaves, just as Janey had said they might do. 'It will have to do for a few days until we can find something better,' said Stefek.

The main problem was Ghost, who was sure to bark loudly if anyone came near. He barked now, as he heard them returning.

'He is a danger to us,' said Stefek. But they both knew they had to keep him because of Janey.

They sat down to study the map carefully.

'It should not be hard to find that place,' Tadek said.

Stefek nodded and looked thoughtful.

Tadek picked up a stick and began to scratch the ground with it, in a careless sort of way.

'I know what you are thinking, Stefek,' he said slowly.

Stefek nodded again. The twins very often knew one another's thought.

'We have to admit it,' said Stefek. 'It would be wrong if we did not. He kept his promise. He did not trick us.'

'Not yet, anyway,' Tadek muttered.

'I do not think you are being fair,' Stefek told him sternly.

'Why not?' said Tadek, jerking his head up and throwing the stick away.

'If he had planned to trick us it would have been a good time, with all that mist lying around. But he brought no one else with him. And when he thought we were not there yet, he was going to leave the map for us and go away.'

Tadek grunted. 'What does that prove?'

'That was a dangerous thing for him to do,' Stefek pointed out. 'Think what might have happened if the Germans had found it instead of us. They would have wanted to know who left it there and why.'

Tadek picked up a stone and tossed it across the quarry. It hit a big boulder and the noise echoed.

'And that is dangerous, too!' said Stefek.

'I'm sorry,' Tadek muttered. He put his head down and ran his fingers through his hair. Then he straightened up again and spoke in a firm voice. 'I have to wait till we go to rescue Janey,' he said. 'If she is in that place and there is no trick, then I will say that I was wrong. I will say that I do not hate all the Germans, for one of them at least is a good man. I will say that, Stefek, but it will not be an easy thing for me to say.'

Chapter 19

It was four in the afternoon. The twins had
been prowling around for hours outside the
house where Janey was a prisoner. But the
rescue was proving to be very difficult.

The house was entirely surrounded by a
wall which was more than a wall, for it was
made of other buildings. These seemed to be
stables and storehouses and servants' houses.
There was only one way in—through an
archway at the front which had a kind of
tower built over it. And of course the
archway was guarded by soldiers.

To make matters worse, the fields around
this outer wall were flat and open, like most
of the countryside there. The boys had not
been able to get close. They had been forced
to crawl along ditches or behind bushes at
least a field away. And they had learned
nothing except that this was a good place to
keep prisoners in.

Now they were holding a council of war in
a ditch beside the narrow cobbled road that
led to the archway.

'We might go in with fruit to sell, as we did
at the town hall,' Stefek suggested. But he
was not at all surprised when Tadek shook

his head. They both knew it was not wise to try the same thing again, for the Germans might have forced Janey to talk about that.

'Could we climb over the roof of one of these houses at night?' said Tadek.

Stefek thought this would be easy enough, for there were drain pipes here and there. But what then? They needed to know where Janey was being kept. How could they find out?

'You need to have wings and be invisible,' said Tadek gloomily. Then all at once he whispered: 'Listen!'

A big truck was lumbering along the road, coming towards the house. It was moving slowly, because the road was really too narrow for it and the trees brushed against its sides.

'I'm going in!' said Tadek urgently. 'I'll climb into the back of that truck as it passes. You must stay out here. I'll find out where she is.'

'Idiot!' Stefek whispered. 'They'll capture you too, just like the lieutenant said.'

'Even if they do, I'll get a signal to you somehow. That's why you must stay outside. Watch for my signal!'

The truck had almost reached them.

'Don't go!' said Stefek, trying to hold Tadek back.

'I must!' he answered. 'It's the only way. We could sit here for ever.'

He shook off Stefek's arm and ran out behind the truck. There was a metal plate to stand on, below the tailboard. Tadek was just tall enough to get a foot on the plate and grab the board above it. Stefek watched unhappily while his brother heaved himself into the truck and disappeared.

The truck was carrying a load of sacks and boxes. Tadek crawled behind a sack and curled up there. It was a very rough ride. A sudden jolt on a bad bit of road made him hit his chin on the floorboards and bite his tongue so that it bled.

A second later the truck stopped and he heard the voices of the guards and the driver. At once he forgot about his sore jaw and his bleeding tongue, for this was the worst moment. If the guards searched the truck they would certainly find him. He longed to be able to understand what they were saying.

He heard feet walking along beside the truck and his body grew tense. The tailboard rattled. Then the feet walked away again while a voice shouted something. The driver shouted in reply and put the truck into gear. They rolled under the archway.

Tadek crawled quickly to the back and risked a look. He had to decide whether to jump down while the truck was still moving, or wait till it stopped. If he waited till it stopped they might begin to unload at once and then there would be no hope for him. It would be better to jump, if they passed close to any place where he could hide.

They were driving on a path which ran between the outer walls and a square garden with a thick clipped hedge around it. The hedge was too thick to crawl through, but at one point it was broken by a tall tree.

As they passed the tree, Tadek scrambled over the tailboard and dropped to the ground. He staggered and fell, but was up again in an instant and running for the gap between the tree and the hedge. If anyone had been looking out from the stable behind him he would surely have been seen. But no shout came.

He crouched in the shadow where the hedge ended and he looked into the garden. It was a good garden for hiding in. There were many shrubs with paths wandering among them. There were sunken paved places and little stone walls and summer-houses. There were big trees.

Tadek smiled.

Until night came Tadek hid in the garden. Then he moved out and began to scout around.

The shutters were not closed and light streamed from the windows of a big room at the front of the house. Tadek crept towards it and peeped in. Four men were sitting there, drinking coffee and sipping brandy from big fat glasses. Only one of them was in army uniform. Tadek guessed that the others were members of the Gestapo.

He could learn nothing by watching them so he did not waste time. While he lay in the garden, he had asked himself where they would be likely to keep a prisoner. In one of the upstairs rooms, he thought—a room with bars on the windows, perhaps, if there was one. As he went around the house looking for such a room, he passed close to two little windows that were almost level with his shoulder, but he paid no attention to them, for his eyes were scanning the upper storeys.

He found no room with bars. But at the back of the house there was a room, high up, with windows that were no more than narrow slits. These seemed promising. Tadek found a drain pipe and began to climb.

He was a very good climber, so that he was soon able to reach a little stone ledge not far below the windows. The ledge was only about 15 cm wide, however, and he realised that it would not be easy to move along it, for there was nothing to hold on to. It was terrifying to look down at the drop to the ground. He hesitated. Then he thought of Janey shut up behind these windows—and he thought of the Germans. He took a deep breath and began to move along the ledge very cautiously.

The distance to the sill was no more than a metre or two but it seemed a very long time before he reached the window and peered through it. Inside there was total darkness. He could see nothing.

The next problem was to get inside. He took out his knife, to see if he could force the window open. He was not very hopeful about this but, before he even had time to try, something happened which gave him such a fright that he very nearly fell backwards off the sill. A big white face suddenly appeared behind the window-panes.

When he had recovered his balance, Tadek found that he was gazing at the face as if he was hypnotised. He should have been trying to get away along the ledge again. Instead he stayed there like a trapped mouse waiting for the cat to pounce. A hand came up beside the face. The window opened. The hand reached out and pulled him in.

As his eyes got used to the darkness of the room, Tadek stood looking up at the man who had captured him. The man was not wearing uniform—in fact he had an open-necked shirt on. Tadek thought this was a little strange, but he supposed that even the

secret police wore open-necked shirts sometimes.

The man said something which Tadek could not understand, but it seemed to be in French, not German. Tadek opened his mouth to say that he did not speak French, then he changed his mind. Best to say nothing at all when you were in the hands of the enemy.

The man spoke again, obviously demanding an answer. Tadek stayed silent. The man scratched his head. Then, instead of dragging Tadek out of the room and down the stairs, or hitting him, or even just putting the light on to take a closer look at the boy he had captured, he did something quite unexpected. He sat down—and not on a chair, but on the floor! As he did so, there was a little sound of clinking metal.

By now, Tadek could see quite well inside the room. He looked down and was amazed to find that the man's ankles were chained together. It took him only a second more to understand. This was not a German! Like Janey, this man was a prisoner!

Tadek crouched down at once and began to talk.

'Do you speak English?' he said.

The man looked very surprised, but he nodded. 'A little,' he said with a very strong French accent. 'You are English, boy?'

'No, Polish,' said Tadek, not taking time to explain anything. 'Listen, I am trying to rescue a girl who is a prisoner here—an English girl. Have you seen her?'

The man nodded again.

'Yes, I think. When they bring me yesterday. A little girl with a brown dress?'

'That's right!' cried Tadek eagerly. 'Where is she, then?'

The man shook his head. 'I not know. I think ... they take her down below. Down low.'

'Down below!' said Tadek. 'I must look for her!' And he got to his feet and turned quickly towards the window. But the man spoke again: 'Boy!'

Tadek turned back. The man spread his arms wide with the palms of his hands turned up. Then he pointed to his chained feet.

'I, too, am prisoner,' he said gently.

Tadek felt ashamed. 'I ... we ...' he said. Then: 'Listen, my brother is outside. When I have found out where Janey is, we'll make plans and we'll try to help you, too.'

The man smiled. 'I thank you,' he said. Then he added: 'I tell you, be quick for the girl. I hear something. I think they will take her soon to Germany.'

Chapter 20

When Tadek had gone, Stefek felt very unhappy. He was worried about his brother but at the same time he envied him. For Tadek had found something important to do, while Stefek was left sitting miserably in a ditch feeling helpless.

He sucked a piece of grass and tried to think of some useful plan. There was no point in going in there too. Tadek was right—one of them had to stay outside meanwhile. But there must be something he could do that would help. In the end, he decided to go all round the outside of the wall once again, looking at it closely and thinking about ways to get in and out, for perhaps that would be useful later on.

When he had gone about three-quarters of the way, he had still not managed to think of anything new and he was feeling more miserable than ever. It was then, as he paddled across a stream, crouching low so as not to be seen, that the idea came to him. He suddenly remembered that he had crossed another stream on the other side, and the question rose in his mind: *was* it another stream? If it was the same stream, then probably it flowed right through the grounds!

He climbed out quickly and tried to follow the course of the stream with his eyes. Yes! It did seem to go right to the wall. And where it passed through the wall perhaps a boy—and a girl—might pass too.

Stefek fought with himself about whether he should wait till it was dark. He was very tempted to follow the stream at once, hoping that the grass by the edge of it would give him enough cover. But in the end he made himself see that this was foolish. He must not risk everything for the sake of a few hours. He lay and waited, chewing grass endlessly.

When darkness came at last, he made up for the delay by moving swiftly, running lightly over the fields. The moon had not risen. The night was warm and still.

He had one bad fright as he passed a bush and almost ran into a great dark shape that loomed up immediately in front of him. It turned out to be a cow!

At the wall there was disappointment. The stream ran under a low archway, but heavy iron bars covered the entrance. Water could get through, a boy could not. However, perhaps a boy could find a way of dealing with the problem.

Stefek shook the bars. They held firm. He would need a file. He thought longingly of the tools which they had been forced to leave behind in the old mill. Well, he would just have to go and raid another empty farmhouse.

He took several hours to find what he needed. It was difficult, searching around in the dark, even though he had matches with him. But in the end he came back with a large rusty file, and set to work on one of the bars. He wanted to file it close to the stone and then leave it leaning there, as if it was still securely fixed.

He had been working for about ten minutes when he heard a soft splashing sound coming from inside. He stopped at once. There was no doubt about it! Someone—or something—was moving along the stream. Was it a guard doing an inspection?

Stefek moved quickly to one side and crouched against the wall with his heart beating fast. The splashing sound came nearer. He wondered if he should run further away, but he wanted to know whether it was a guard and whether the filing would be discovered.

The sound came very close and stopped. Someone shook the bars. Then there was a new sound—a tiny little whistle of surprise. Stefek almost laughed out loud. Twins know one another so well that the least sound which one of them makes can be recognised by the other. 'Tadek!' he whispered, as he stepped out from the shadow. And there was Tadek behind the bars with a wide smile of joy on his face.

'Tadek!' said Stefek again, beaming back

at him. 'I thought you were a guard. What happened? Did you find Janey?'

Tadek frowned. 'I'm not sure. Perhaps. There is a sort of cellar with two windows above ground level. I think she may be in there, but I am not quite sure. I could not get the windows open without breaking them and I was afraid to do that because of the noise. Also I think the cellar is deep, with the windows high up, and I did not have a rope that she could climb. And then she might be tied up in there—I don't know. They might have chained her, like the other prisoner.'

'What other prisoner?' Stefek asked at once.

'A man—a Frenchman. I spoke to him. I said we would try to save him, too.'

Now it was Stefek's turn to frown. 'But how could you speak to him if you couldn't get the window open?'

'He was in another room, silly,' Tadek told

him. 'I was in there. His ankles were chained together.'

Stefek shook his head. 'It's much harder if ...'

But Tadek interrupted him. 'Listen, Stefek, listen! It's important. The Frenchman told me something that he heard the Germans saying. They may be planning to take Janey away to Germany.'

'What?' Stefek was horrified. They began at once to make plans.

It was clear that the rescue would have to take place the next night. It would be impossible in the daytime—and the first light of the new day was already beginning to drift up into the sky.

They agreed that Tadek should take the file and get on with the work on the bars. Then he would sleep somewhere for an hour or two. Later he would crawl back into the grounds of the house and keep watch, so that they would know if anything important happened.

Meanwhile Stefek would go back to the quarry to feed Ghost and to fetch more food for themselves, for they had just eaten the last of the biscuits they had brought with them the day before. He would then search for two long pieces of rope and another file and a chisel—or two chisels if he could find them. He would be back as soon as it was dark to meet Tadek.

When all this had been settled, Stefek slipped away across the fields.

Chapter 21

It was evening again. Inside the big house the men of the Gestapo were sitting once more over their coffee and brandy. For them just now life was very good. One of them raised his glass and they all jumped to their feet, gave the Nazi salute and drank a toast to the Führer. Outside, two small dark figures ran quietly through the garden.

The first problem for the twins was how to open the window of the cellar where they hoped to find Janey. In France the windows open down the middle, and the frames are curved at the place where they join, so that it is not possible to get the blade of a knife through.

The twins looked at the putty around the frame. It was old and crumbly, as they had hoped. The best plan was probably to chip the putty away until they could lift one side of the window right out. They set to work as hard as they could with their knives and chisels.

Inside, Janey was curled up asleep. They had given her a mattress to lie on after the first night. She was still afraid of rats, though none had appeared, and now she was dreaming that a very big one was at the door, scratching and scratching, gnawing, trying to get in. She woke with a little scream, sat up, and heard the noise above her head.

For a second, while the dream was still with her, she thought it was a rat at the window. Then she came wide awake, and knew that was nonsense. She jumped to her feet and stared upwards.

At that moment the boys got the right-hand side of the little window out, and Stefek stuck his head through. 'Janey!' he whispered. 'Are you there?'

Janey almost wept for joy.

'Stefek! Tadek!' she whispered back. 'Oh, is it really you?'

'Really us!' Stefek assured her. 'Just a minute!'

He pulled his head out again and thrust the end of a length of rope through the window. The other end was tied firmly over his own right shoulder, with a knot under the left arm to stop it from tightening. 'Now climb it, Janey,' he told her. Janey caught the rope and began to climb.

In the big room at the front of the house the Gestapo man who had questioned Janey drank the last of his brandy, got up from his armchair and stretched himself.

'A pleasant evening,' he said. 'Will anyone walk with me in the garden?'

'Gladly, sir,' said a smaller man with a moustache, rising to his feet. The two of them strolled out on to the terrace.

The twins heard the voices when Janey's head was still about a foot below the window. They looked at each other with an urgent question in their eyes. Should she go back down? They both shook their heads.

'Quick!' Stefek whispered, and they pulled on the rope and reached in to grab Janey's shoulders and heave her through.

The voices were growing louder. The nearest hiding place was a big bush on the other side of the drive. The twins raced for it, with Janey running between them. Peeping out breathlessly from there, they saw two dark shapes turning the corner from the front of the house, about fifteen metres away. A whiff of cigar smoke was carried along on the wind and the end of the cigar glowed red in the darkness as the big Gestapo man drew on it with a sigh of pleasure.

Then the voices grew fainter again as the Germans turned back along the terrace.

Janey was surprised that the twins did not immediately begin to move away.

'What is it?' she asked. 'Can't we go now?'

Tadek pointed towards the back of the house.

'There's another prisoner,' he said. 'A Frenchman. I promised to get him out too.'

'Oh!' said Janey. She was feeling weak and shaky. She longed to get away from that place. But she remembered the Frenchman. She had seen them bringing him in. It was after they had questioned her for the second time, when they were taking her back to the cellar. They had dragged him through the hall and there was blood on his face.

'Yes,' she said. 'Of course. We have to try to save him.'

'I'm going alone,' said Tadek firmly. 'There's no need for more than one of us, and I know where he is. Stefek will take you to our secret way out of here. Wait for us there.'

He peered out cautiously from the bush and ran towards the house again.

The climb up the drainpipe was no harder than before but the walk along the ledge seemed worse. The sight of the Gestapo men in the garden had been upsetting. And when you were easing your way along that ledge you could not look down to see if anyone was coming. You had to keep all of your mind on simply getting along there without falling.

Tadek was sweating by the time he reached the window sill. He drew a breath of relief and tapped gently on the pane. The Frenchman's delight when he saw the file made up for everything; and Tadek had time to rest while the man got rid of his chains. But there was no way to avoid the fact that the journey along the ledge had to be made yet again.

The Frenchman did not like it either. 'Zhut!' he said, as he looked down.

Tadek went first, and he could hear the man's heavy breathing behind him. But when he got as far as the drainpipe he realised that the man was clinging to the wall halfway along, not moving, and for a moment he was afraid something might be badly wrong. Then the man came on again, very slowly. Tadek began to go down.

A German car was parked in the yard, not far from the foot of the drainpipe. Tadek ran to hide behind it as they had arranged, and as soon as the Frenchman reached the ground he did the same. Tadek saw that he was limping.

'Are you all right?' he asked. The man just nodded. 'Then follow me,' Tadek told him.

The Gestapo chief had gone into the house and had said goodnight to the other men. He had even gone up to his room for a while, but he felt restless and he knew he would not sleep. So he came down again and wandered out once more into the garden. This time he did not smoke, and he moved silently, like a big fat white ghost among the shrubs and hedges.

The chief's mind was busy with a problem. He knew that the German armies were very likely to capture Paris before long—Paris, that fabulous city. If he was lucky he would be promoted and sent to an important job there. If he was lucky—*and* if he did his present job well. So he would have to get that stubborn Frenchman to talk, and quickly. As for the girl, she was less important. But still ...

Suddenly he stiffened. There was a noise! Feet on the grass—someone coming! Light feet, moving cautiously. Now why ...? The Gestapo chief drew in behind a bush and waited. Tadek's small figure glided past him.

With one jump the chief had Tadek by the collar. 'So!' he roared in a deep and mighty voice. Then the roar changed to a yell and died away in a grunt as the Frenchman leapt at the chief's throat from behind.

The chief kicked and struggled with his big body but the Frenchman had a firm grip with his right arm. When the chief stopped struggling and went limp, the Frenchman dropped him instantly.

'Come! Quick!' he said to Tadek, and they ran.

Already the whole place was in an uproar, for the chief's cry had been heard. Windows lit up in the house and men came running. But they had no idea what was happening, and they ran wildly here and there.

It took them several minutes to find the

place where the chief was lying. By then the twins and the escaping prisoners were splashing along the stream. And by the time the hunt for them was organized they were already well away over the fields.

Chapter 22

'In here!' whispered the Frenchman, as he opened a wooden gate in a high brick wall. Inside there was a paved yard and you could see the back of a house. It was dark and silent.

'Now,' he said when the gate was shut again, 'there is a car in that garage over there. At least, I very much hope there is. Let's see!'

He spoke in French, for he was in too much of a hurry to struggle with the English words. Janey had to keep explaining to the twins what he had said.

The car was there—a small black Peugeot. The Frenchman smiled.

'So *that* is good,' he said. 'You see, we need a car. It is possible that they may send dogs after us. But dogs cannot follow a car.'

Janey shivered. 'Did they have dogs there?' she said. 'I didn't hear any.'

'I think they did not,' he answered. 'They're not very well organized yet. They may bring dogs from somewhere else, though.'

He reached inside the car and brought out an envelope and a torch. 'They will certainly search for us very thoroughly,' he went on, as he shut the garage door again. 'But they will not expect us to have a car. I hid it here before they caught me.'

'Where will we go in the car?' Janey asked him.

'To the place where my wife is—and where I have friends. Now, let's think carefully. They will be looking for a man and a little girl. They did not see the boys, did they?'

Janey asked the twins.

'No,' said Tadek, 'except the fat man in the garden.' He paused. 'Did you kill him?'

The Frenchman looked at the three faces for a moment in silence. Then he said 'Yes,' very abruptly in English, and went on to speak at once in French again. 'Right! The girl must change into a boy! We are going into the house now. We must not put lights on, remember.'

He had a key to the back door. From somewhere upstairs he fetched grey trousers, a yellow shirt and a dark blue woollen jacket. 'Try these,' he said to Janey.

They were a good fit. The Frenchman switched on the torch for a moment, looked at her and nodded.

'This is my brother's house,' he explained. 'These clothes belong to my nephew. I thought he was about the right size. He will be happy to let you borrow them. Now, scissors! Where will they be?'

They found scissors in a kitchen drawer.

'I am not a good hairdresser by daylight,'

said the Frenchman with a grin, 'and I am even worse in the dark. Come over here by the window where there is some moonlight now. I will try not to cut your ears off at least! Later my wife will make a better job for you.'

And Janey sat in a patch of moonlight while her long dark hair was clipped away.

'That is not bad, I think,' said the Frenchman when it was done. 'Now you sleep.'

'Sleep?' cried Janey. 'Are we not going in the car?'

'Not yet. There is a rule that no one is allowed to go out at night. It is called a curfew. If we go now, the first German soldiers that we meet on the road will certainly stop us and they might shoot us at

once. If we go when it is light, I think we have a chance.'

'But what if they come here?' Janey asked him. She was thinking about the dogs.

'That is a risk we have to take,' the Frenchman said. 'They did not have many guards in that place. They will send for more soldiers, but they may take some time to arrive. I will keep watch. You will sleep.'

Janey told the twins.

'We will help to keep watch too,' said Tadek at once.

'No,' said the Frenchman, very firmly.

'Why not?'

'I tell you,' said the Frenchman, 'but I tell in French, eh?'

He turned to Janey and explained: 'Even if they come we may be all right, *if* they are not led here by dogs.' He held up one finger in the moonlight. 'And *if* no one comes who can recognize me.' He held up a second finger. 'And *if* three boys are tucked up in their beds, sleeping soundly as children are supposed to be doing at this time of night.' As he spoke he raised a third finger. 'Now,' he said, 'do you understand?'

Janey translated into English, and the twins nodded.

'Also,' said the Frenchman, 'I have a piece of paper which may help us if they come.' But he did not explain what this mysterious piece of paper could be.

Before she climbed into bed, Janey said: 'Please, what is your name?'

'Ah! I forgot to tell you. My name is

Gaston. If they come, you call me Uncle Gaston. But say as little as possible. And tell the twins to say nothing at all.'

Chapter 23

They did not come. Gaston woke the children when it was time and gave them biscuits and black coffee. It was all he could find in the house.

Janey peeped in a mirror and thought that she looked very funny with short hair. She made a face at herself and stuck out her tongue.

After breakfast, Gaston gave her a beret to put on her head so that no one would notice how badly the hair had been cut. He pulled a beret on to his own head also and drew it forward to cover a big cut on his brow near the line of his hair. Janey noticed that he was looking very pale, apart from the darkness of the skin around his eyes.

'Now,' he said, 'we go!'

He drove the car out of the yard and turned it towards the north-west.

For ten miles the road was completely quiet. During this time Gaston got Janey to tell him the story of how she came to be with the twins, and how the Germans had captured her. She noticed that he seemed to be very interested to hear about her father. He kept asking questions about him. What was his work? Why did he not leave France along with Janey?

Janey answered as well as she could.

'You do not know what exactly he was going to do when he stayed behind?' Gaston asked her.

'No,' said Janey.

Gaston looked thoughtful and was silent for a while. But as they rounded the next corner, he spoke again. 'Look!' he said.

They were coming towards a crossroads. And a German motorcycle was driving slowly towards the same crossing from a road on the right.

'Now,' said Gaston, 'I expect they will stop us. We must not seem to be worried. Sit very quietly and leave it to me.'

The Germans began to move faster. It was clear that the car had been seen.

The motorcycle reached the crossroads first, swung round, and stopped in the middle. The man in the sidecar pointed his machine gun straight towards the car, while the driver held up his hand, making a signal: Halt! Gaston slowed the car down and stopped it a few yards away.

The driver got off his cycle and strolled over to the car as if he was not in any kind of hurry. He was a big dark man with a large nose and very fierce-looking eyes. He said something in German and peered suspiciously through the open window.

Gaston answered him, also in German. Then he took a piece of paper from his pocket and handed it to the soldier. The man looked at it, turned it over, looked at it again. He seemed to hesitate. He was frowning.

Just at that moment, a big black car with a motorcycle escort swept into sight from the direction in which Gaston and the children had been heading.

The German soldier jumped back and ran towards his cycle, shouting something as he went. He moved the cycle to the roadside, but the machine gunner swung his gun round so that it was still aiming all the time at Gaston's car. The big car stopped.

It was a car with an open roof, just like the ones Janey had seen outside her father's house. And, as usual, there were two German officers sitting in the back of it.

One of the officers shouted something and the driver of the motorcycle hurried across and saluted. The children could see him handing over Gaston's piece of paper. They could hear Gaston drawing in his breath between his teeth.

The first officer read the paper and passed it to the second officer. The second officer said something and gave the paper back to the first officer, who gave it to the motor-cycle driver. The driver stepped back and saluted again as the car drove away. Gaston let his breath out.

When the big car had disappeared, the soldier came back to Gaston and handed the piece of paper through the window. Then he moved a foot or two away, stuck out his right arm and shouted: 'Heil Hitler!' Gaston stuck out his right arm and shouted 'Heil Hitler!'

back at him. The German signalled to them to drive on.

When they were well away from the cross-roads, Janey said, 'What is the piece of paper, Gaston?'

'It is a document signed by a senior German officer saying that I have given much help to the German army and that I am to be allowed to pass freely.'

Janey began to say this in English for the twins. She got as far as the words 'signed by', then she blushed and stammered and stopped. Gaston glanced sideways at her and grinned. 'But of course the German did not really sign it,' he explained. 'It is a forgery— a good forgery, made by my friends for me to use at just such a time as this.'

'Why did they not find it when you were a prisoner?' Janey asked.

'I did not have it with me. It was in the car. You see, I knew that if they caught me doing what I was going to do, then they would certainly not believe this bit of paper.'

'What were you going to do?'

'I was going to blow up a bridge,' said Gaston, 'But I did not manage it.' He shrugged his shoulders. 'Another time!'

Chapter 24

'So we must get you to the coast and put you on a fishing boat that will take you back to England,' said Gaston.

Janey looked down and said nothing. Gaston's wife, Claire, leaned forward, speaking gently. 'It is the best thing now. It is the only thing to do now. Don't you see?'

They were sitting round the table in the kitchen of Gaston's house. Light from the setting sun was gleaming on Claire's dark hair, which was twisted up at the back of her head. Everyone was looking at Janey.

'All right,' she said slowly. 'I will go back to England now. But only if I can do something else first.'

'What is that?' Gaston asked her.

'I will go if I can get my dog first and bring him too.'

'Your dog?' said Gaston, in surprise.

Janey had not spoken about Ghost since their escape, though she had thought about him often. Now she turned to the twins.

'When did you feed Ghost last?' she said.

'Yesterday,' Tadek told her.

'Did you leave him tied up in the quarry?'

'We had to,' said Stefek. 'You know that.'

'I know that.'

Janey spoke to Gaston again.

'They left him tied up. If we don't fetch him soon he'll die. I can't go away and leave him. I just can't!'

Gaston smiled and put out his hand and rumpled her ragged-looking hair. 'I understand,' he said. 'I did not know about your dog. Of course you can't leave him to die. We'll fetch him and he shall go too.'

The movement of Gaston's hand reminded Claire that she had a job to do.

'I will cut your hair properly for you now, before you go,' she said. 'Come over here, Janey!' She said Janey's name in a funny French sort of way, so that it sounded like 'Zhanee'.

'Are we going tonight?' Janey asked. She had not expected to leave so soon.

'Yes, when it gets dark,' Gaston told her.

'But what about the curfew? You said we had to move by daylight,' Janey reminded him.

'That was when we were in the car. Tonight we are going to walk across the fields. We are going to a meeting with some of my friends.'

Janey explained this to the twins. It was hard for them to sit there, not understanding. They had both decided by now that they were going to learn as many languages as possible so that they would be able to go all over the world and always know what people were saying.

'How's that?' said Claire, holding up a mirror. 'Better, I think.'

'Very good,' said Gaston. 'All the girls would want to have their hair like that if they could see you.'

Claire turned to the twins. 'Now,' she said, waving her scissors and speaking in English, 'it is time for boys, no?'

It was true that the boys' hair was beginning to grow over their ears. They grinned and went, one by one, to have it clipped short again.

'Gaston,' said Janey, 'why are we going to this meeting?'

'Because my friends will be able to find a way to get you to the coast—and to get your dog, don't worry!' he added quickly. 'There are five of us in our group. We all decided not to go away when the Germans came. We decided to stay and fight them, just as you did.' He paused. Janey saw that he stiffened his body. 'It will be a hard fight, and there are not many of us yet. But soon there will be more, and more. And one day we will throw the Germans right out of France again. You'll see!'

Tadek had been watching and listening closely and he seemed somehow to understand this. 'And out of Poland!' he said fiercely, with his eyes shining.

They walked for nearly two hours across the dark fields. Now and again they heard planes in the sky, but they met no one. Janey found herself remembering her first journey and

179

she began to wish she could take Plodder back to England with her too. But she knew that it was impossible. It was lucky that Plodder could look after himself, not like Ghost.

'You see that line of poplar trees?' Gaston whispered. 'The house we are going to is just beyond them. Not far now! Are you tired?'

'No,' said Janey, telling a lie.

There was not a chink of light showing through the shutters as they came near.

'They have put heavy curtains in behind,' Gaston explained. 'Now, there is a special knock. It is like the first line of our national anthem. Listen!' And he tapped on the door: ra—*tat*—ra—*tat*—*tat*—*tat*—*tat*—*tat*—ra—*tat*, humming the tune softly as he did so.

They heard feet moving inside and the sound of a bolt being drawn. Then the door opened and they stepped quickly into the dark hall.

'Gaston!' cried a man's voice. 'Thank God! We thought you were dead!'

He switched on the light as soon as the door was safely closed again. He was a young man—not more than twenty probably—very big and strong, with huge hands.

'Who are the children?' he asked, in a voice that sounded surprised and rather disapproving.

'They rescued me,' said Gaston. 'I'd still be in a Gestapo prison but for them.'

'They rescued you!' The man's voice was more surprised than ever now, but very much less disapproving. 'Then they are heroes!' He stood up straight and tall, with his head close to the ceiling, and saluted them. 'Welcome, young heroes!' he said. His elbow caught the flex of the light and set the shade swinging from side to side.

'Philippe?' said Gaston.

'What?' said the young man, grinning down at him.

'Has Gérard come?'

'Yes, he's here. In you go!'

Philippe led the way into a sitting room. He had to duck his head a little to get through the doorway. Tadek thought that he would like to be as big as that one day.

'Here is our dear friend Gaston,' said the young man in a clear, strong voice. 'And he brings with him three young heroes.' He said it as if he were a herald announcing visitors at the court of a king. It would have sounded

right if he had lifted a trumpet to his lips and blown a fanfare.

Janey was the first to go into the room. Four men were sitting there, at a round table, with wine glasses in front of them. The one with his back to the door twisted his chair round, and they all looked at her through the smoke that hung in the air. She felt bewildered and shy. She looked from one man to another, blinking a little and feeling her legs aching.

Then her heart gave a great jump and she stared at one of them, forgetting everything else, not quite believing what she saw.

'Daddy!' she cried, and ran towards him.

Chapter 25

It took Janey's father more than a second to recognize his daughter in her trousers and boy's jacket and short boy's hair. It took both of them longer still to believe that this could be true. The others watched with smiling faces as they hugged one another.

'I thought so!' Gaston was saying. 'When you told me about your father, I thought so.'

'Why did you not tell me, then?' Janey cried.

'Because I was not sure. I knew there was an Englishman who was helping to organize groups of fighters like ours, but I had never met him. I knew he was supposed to come to this meeting tonight. But I did not know his name. We called him Gérard, but this is just a code name, you see. I didn't want to make you hope in case it was not your father after all.'

Then everyone began to speak at once, some of them in French and some in English and some of them translating from one language into the other. The first thing Janey's father wanted to know was why she was not safely home in England. When she explained how Martin had gone for help and had not returned, her father sighed.

'Poor Martin!' he said. 'Something bad must have happened to him. He would never have left you like that.'

'I knew that,' said Janey. 'I always knew that.'

'How did you manage then?' her father asked. 'What did you do? You met these boys?'

'No, no, that was much later. I went back to St Quentin first.'

'All alone?' Her father's voice sounded amazed.

'No,' she said. 'I wasn't alone. You see, I had a horse and I had a dog with me. He's called Ghost—and he's tied up in a quarry, and we have to fetch him.'

So then they planned that Philippe would go to the quarry next morning with one of the twins and find Ghost and bring him back. And Janey went on to tell them how she had met the boys and they had decided to fight the Germans.

Her father listened quietly to the story of the attack on the town hall of St Quentin. Then he said, 'That was a brave thing to do and I am proud of you, even though I would never have let you try it.'

Gaston had been listening. He understood English much better than he could speak it. He said now in French: 'But if they had not tried it I would still be in prison. And the Germans might have forced me to tell them about our group in the end, you know. I hope not, but I cannot be sure that I would have been strong enough to stay silent.'

Janey's father nodded. 'I realise that,' he said. 'But I still don't know how it happened that the children rescued you.'

'Ah, well,' said Gaston, 'the Germans caught your daughter and they put her in the prison that I was in. Then these boys came to get her out, and they got me out too.'

Janey's father, still struggling to understand it all, turned to the twins: 'How did you know where the Germans had taken Janey then? How were you able to find that out?'

Stefek looked at Tadek and waited for him to speak. Tadek flushed, but he spoke firmly: 'A German officer helped us.'

'Did he now? Tell me about that,' said Janey's father, leaning forward and looking very interested. All the others stopped talking and listened too. Even Janey did not know this bit of the story.

'Yes,' said Tadek. 'He gave us a map and he told us he had actually seen Janey in the prison. And I promised my brother that if it was not a trick I would say that I do not hate all Germans any more, for one of them at least is a good man.' He stood up very straight. 'I say it now. I do not hate all Germans any more, for one of them at least is a good man.'

'I knew he was a good man,' said Janey. 'I liked him.'

Gaston filled a glass of wine and picked it up.

'We should all remember,' he murmured.

'Do you know the man's name?'

But the children shook their heads. He had never told them his name.

'You know,' said Janey thoughtfully, 'it's true what Gaston said—that we'd never have met him if the Germans hadn't caught me. And if we hadn't met Gaston, I probably wouldn't have found out where you were, Daddy.'

'That's right,' said her father. 'Probably not.'

He looked around the circle of faces. Everyone was quiet now.

'Before you came this evening,' he went on, 'we were talking about what to do next. And we had just decided to try to get in touch with London. It's about time for that now, isn't it, Gaston?'

Gaston nodded. 'I agree.'

'So we were planning that I should try to get across the Channel very soon. What do you say to that?'

'Yes!' cried Janey, before Gaston could answer. Gaston smiled and said 'Yes' too.

'So we'll all go, Janey—you and me and the boys. It may not be easy, but we'll find a way.'

'And Ghost, too!' said Janey.

'And Ghost, too,' her father agreed.

They went to bed very soon afterwards, for everyone was tired by that time, except Philippe, who never seemed to get tired at all.

Janey was given a tiny room up in the attic. Her father came to say goodnight and he sat for a moment on the edge of the bed, looking at her. 'There's just one more thing, Janey,' he said, speaking very seriously. 'You do understand, don't you, that I'll probably have to come back to France again before long?'

'Yes,' said Janey, 'I do understand.'

And she did.

He smiled, and kissed her. She was asleep before he had closed the door.